the ballad of
two sisters

a novel

Darci Schummer

——For my father, Jerome Francis Schummer (August 14, 1938 – August 22, 2018), and my sisters, the true loves of my life.

the ballad of
two sisters

a novel

Chapter 1: The End

In the basement of the Bells & Stone Funeral Home where the dead were embalmed and staged, the Mortician pushed play on his portable CD player and stared at a picture of Helen and Stella. He paused for a second, listening to the music. No, it wasn't right. Billie Holiday wasn't right. It was Ella they needed, the brightness of her voice. He went back to the player and changed the CD. Then, fingertips at the very edges, he examined the photo first directly under the florescent light of the preparation room and next in the glow that radiated around it. He held it so close to his face he thought he could see the individual strands of the women's perfectly coiffed hair and then far enough from his face so that Helen and Stella looked like women he had gazed upon only from across crowded rooms or across crowded streets. In the photo, the women were standing in front of a glass-doored china cabinet full of plates, bric-a-brac, decorative spoons. Their arms were intertwined, their neutral-colored skirts and flowered blouses neatly pressed. A point of light shone between them, the nearly invisible shadow of their photographer behind it. As the music played, the Mortician held the photo against his chest for a moment, then searched it for something he had not yet seen. This time he noticed the way Helen's head leaned slightly toward Stella. *You dear women*, he thought, *you wouldn't have wanted it any other way.*

The sisters, ages 76 and 78 respectively, had died on the same day.

He started the CD over, put on his gloves, gown, and mask, and began his work, regarding the women as he would have his own sisters. It was how he treated all his clients. The first thing he did was close their eyes; it was better to start that way, he thought. He mixed the necessary fluids, then placed modesty cloths over the gray hair of their sexes, avoiding eye contact with their breasts as much as he could without affecting the quality of his work. He hummed while washing their bodies and gently massaging and flexing their arms and legs to eliminate rigor mortis. When he stumbled upon the sisters' tattoos—blurs of black lines on their wrinkled torsos—he dabbed thick lotion on them, which made them grow brighter, more defined. "Ah, birds," he said, pulling the sisters' skin taut. "What is the story behind these? I know there must be a story, a good one." He smiled, thinking of the secret their skin held—a secret now just between the women and him. He reviewed the women's picture again before setting their features. He wanted the faces of his clients to look natural; it was such sensitive work. Carefully, he sutured their jaws shut, first placing cotton in their mouths to fill the hollowness that age and death had gifted.

Occasionally, like any doctor or dentist would during a procedure, he stopped to ask each woman how she was doing. "Are you comfortable? Can I do anything to make this better?" he said, waiting for a response that wouldn't come. Still, it made him feel better to ask.

After remembering how Helen's head had leaned toward her older sister, he was careful to handle her with extreme delicacy, for he could sense she was the more fragile of the two. While a machine replaced her blood with embalming fluid, he massaged her again, distributing the fluid throughout her body, patting the top of her head occasionally as if to say, *It's almost over, sweetheart.* Caring for Stella, he imagined she would have suffered through the process sighing but perhaps cracking a one-liner here and there at his expense. He chuckled a few times imagining the undertaker jokes she probably knew, her face flush in his mind.

Next came the part he disliked most—cavity embalming. He hated making another incision, hated puncturing the organs, but he had learned to do it quickly, had learned to temper his dislike for it. So he worked through the process, not engaging with the women, distancing himself from the task. When he finished, the women were more lifelike. They looked more like the women from the photograph, and he felt better.

Finally, it was time to bring the sisters' faces to life. This, perhaps, was his favorite part of preparing the decedents: whereas they had been lifeless canvasses, when the work with his palette was done, they were vivified, the dimensions of animacy restored to them. He was a masterful painter, a constant critic of color. Never did he use one lipstick or blush straight out of the package; rather, each was blended so that no two people ever wore the exact same shade. It was the least he could do for them, this final act. For Helen, he used subdued pinks. She was paler than Stella, and the picture showed that her cheeks were rosy, a quality that belied her age. For Stella, he used deeper tones, hues tinged with orange, which complimented her olive skin. Based on their skin alone, it was hard to believe they were sisters, but after he had vivified them, he could see the ineffable quality they shared. He rolled his chair back to the edge of the room and propped an elbow on the green Formica countertop.

"Did I do well, ladies?" he asked.

That evening, as the Mortician and funeral director looked on, the small number of the sisters' family members who were still alive said the usual things, slanting their lives into unadulterated sunlight. It all seemed so orchestrated to the Mortician that he felt he knew the women better than their family ever had.

"They were good aunts, good friends, good...well, good people," an old man said, staring at note cards. He cleared his throat and shuffled them, having lost his place. "And," he stammered, "And...we were all a damn sight lucky to know them." He fumbled through the rest of his speech. After, he shook his head and took a seat next to a gray-haired woman who, in a consolatory gesture, ran her manicured nails across the back of his neck.

The Mortician began to pace. Why did he even bother attending the funerals? Every one of them was a worse incarnation of the last. They were full of disingenuousness, devoid of actual emotion. There was no wail, no desperation. He had done all this work to give families, friends, lovers the opportunity to howl loud and long, to crawl on their knees and beg God and Satan to stop the endless game and give them back their dead.

"It's not right," he mumbled.

"What?" the funeral director said, appearing behind him.

"It's not right," he said louder.

"Shhh…"

"It isn't. I know those women better than they do. These people aren't even saying anything worthwhile."

"What did I tell you? If you keep getting this—this agitated, you can't come up here anymore. Understand?"

"You don't understand."

"What don't I understand?" The funeral director led him by the arm around the corner, out of the guests' line of sight.

"It's just a show."

"It's supposed to be a show."

"No one up there is being honest."

The funeral director positioned himself so that he stood between the Mortician and the guests. "How many times are we going to go through this before you have to get another job?"

"As many times as it takes for you to understand my point."

"Listen——you know what I know about you. Do we have to have the conversation?"

The Mortician ran a hand through his hair and looked down at his feet. It was the same conversation he had in Florida, in Texas, in Georgia, in Mississippi. The reason he had moved north was to escape those conversations, which were a steel wreckage consuming so much space in his mind that it had taken all the self-control he could summon just to present himself as a new man, a new mortician in Illinois.

During his interview at Bells & Stone, "I do excellent work," he had said. "I treat them like my own family."

"That's what your references said about you," the funeral director replied. "But they also seemed to have some concerns about your level of involvement with the families. I share those concerns as well."

The Mortician's jaw tensed. "Concerns?" But he knew the concerns well. He could still picture that last funeral in Florida: a wife coffined in her wedding dress, a Rembrandt of vivification. Her husband, dry-eyed, wore a white t-shirt with yellowed arm pits and liquor on his breath. Their children were weeping raw, completely true in grief. The young girl had wrapped her arms around herself and was rocking back and forth with each new wave of sob. The boy stared at the floor, continually running his hands down the length of his khaki-covered thighs. "Quit crying," the husband had said. "Just quit your crying. It won't do you any good. She's gone."

The husband thought only the three of them were in the room, but he had failed to realize that the Mortician, anger rising, was behind him. Watching the man stealing his children's right to grieve, to partake in a necessary ritual infuriated the Mortician. The theft endangered the children, for how would they move on if they did not first purge themselves of all that darkness?

"It won't do you any good," the husband growled. "You hear me?"

After he said it, the Mortician was upon him, and even now the Mortician did not clearly remember what had happened, just that he and the man were suddenly outside the room alone, and the man was on the ground, and...

"Did you hear what I just said?" the funeral director snapped.

"Yes. I heard you."

"Do you like your job, son?"

The funeral director was always calling him son, although the Mortician, age 35, wasn't sure the funeral director was old enough to be his father.

"Listen, I know you like your job, son. You're good at it. You want to keep it? Then you need to let go a bit now, don't you? You deal with the dead. I deal with the living. That was our agreement."

"Right," the Mortician muttered, sequestering every last thread of his anger. "Right," he repeated. Then he turned and walked away from the funeral director, away from Stella and Helen and the guests, but he walked slowly, listening to another subpar speech get quieter and quieter until he was in the preparation room again. He inhaled deeply, the sound of his own breathing the only noise, the room, devoid of the two sisters, as silent and insulated as a tomb.

Chapter 2: War

Though Helen was a young girl during World War II, battles fought with airplanes and tanks and atomic bombs across the sea would not shape her; rather, battles fought in her parents' two-bedroom apartment in Chicago affixed themselves to her heart. Helen and her sister Stella, who was less than two years older, often woke in the middle of the night to insults firing out of their parents' mouths. Mornings after, Helen's mother hid her face; her back was always toward Helen, but when she had to turn partway to hand over a bagged lunch, Helen saw purple beneath one of her eyes, a red split down her lip, or some other remnant of violent engagement. She knew to avoid her father that day, for the days after a fight he rarely spoke or looked at any of the females he lived with, as though he knew he had wronged all three of them but did not have the strength to admit his transgressions. On those days, some extra sweet always appeared in both Helen and Stella's lunches, a freshly baked cookie or piece of pie. Neither Helen nor Stella had any appetite for it and would often trade it to a classmate for something else——something store bought. As she ate what she had bartered for, Helen swore never to be like her mother and never to marry a man like her father.

At school, she trailed Stella like a fraying ribbon. Having no real friends, she played and ate lunch with Stella and Stella's friends, a rag tag group of girls with downturned eyes and stringy hair.

"Don't you know they'll tease us if we're always together?" Stella said as they got off the train and walked toward Darwin Elementary one morning. "Everyone will think we're freaks if we just hang out with each other. You have to find your own friends. Start talking to people."

Tears welled in Helen's eyes. Her hands and arms tingled like they often did when she sat in the classroom. Unable to pay attention to the teacher's lesson, her mind galloped across the landscape of what had happened at home the night before or what would happen that night.

"You have to stop crying at school, too. You're in 4th grade now. 4th graders don't cry at school anymore."

Helen looked at Stella, but Stella looked straight ahead. Her cheeks were red, and she kicked a rock as they walked. "I'm sorry," Helen whimpered.

"It's OK. I'm just telling you."

For the rest of that day, Helen did as Stella asked, forcing herself not to look for her sister at lunch. As soon as she was dismissed for recess, she ran to the swings, pent-up thoughts diffusing through her muscles. She pumped her legs hard, soaring up and up until at the highest point in her swinging the playground vanished, and she felt as though she might simply disappear into the sky itself. In the rapture of her motion, she did not notice the group of girls gathering around below her. When she did see them, she automatically slowed her pace, a primal voice whispering *danger* inside her head. Then came the sudden jolt as a girl on each side of her grabbed the swing's chains, knocking her off her windy throne. Helen knelt in the snowy gravel beneath the swing, her palms stinging, tears forming in her eyes. But she did not cry out. *4th graders don't cry,* she heard Stella say.

She hoped she could simply get up and walk away. When she stood, however, Margaret Anderson, a girl universally feared and followed by all 4th graders, was in front of her. Helen put her shoulder forward and tried to pass, but Margaret blocked her.

"Stay off these swings," she said.

The buttons on Margaret's winter coat strained across her stomach and her skinny long legs pointed slightly inward at the knees. Helen looked into the girl's narrowed black eyes, over which a single lock of brown hair sailed in the early winter wind. At first she was afraid, but her knees were burning and her palms were stinging and last night her father and mother had argued over some missing money until her father stormed out of the house.

"I'll look for you where the bums hang out under the tracks, you son of a bitch," her mother had yelled. "We'd be better off if you'd hurry up and drink yourself to death." Then she turned on the radio and chained smoked cigarettes. Helen breathed in smoke to the sound of her mother humming, unable to sleep until the blanket of darkness thinned to a worn sheet. She never heard her father come home.

"Looks like your dad's taking the day off work," their mother said as she absently fed the girls Corn Flakes in the morning. "Just another day off work." Helen's father worked as a neighborhood handyman, picking up jobs steadily for weeks or even months at a time and then turning unreliable on a whim. "Wonder how many customers he's going to lose this time." Helen concentrated on her cereal, which was getting soggy, and neither she nor Stella said anything.

Thinking about all that made defiance rise in Helen, and she didn't care about Margaret Anderson who everyone said was awful behind her back anyway.

"Why?" she said, looking at the girl straight on. "Why should I?"

"Because I said to."

"No."

"Excuse me?"

"I said NO. I won't do it."

"Listen, stupid, these are our swings after lunch," Margaret said, her finger pointing to the girls standing behind her.

Helen looked from Margaret's eyes to the eyes of the other girls. All of them were steeled against her.

"I know about you," Margaret said.

"What are you talking about?"

"My mom saw your mom getting handouts at St. Luke's. Is that where your ugly dress came from?"

Helen liked this dress. She did not know where it had come from, just that it had been on her bed one day after school. It was brown and white plaid with gathers at the waist. The collar had a blue bow, and the fabric was soft and warm.

"What's wrong with my dress?" she said.

The girls laughed.

"It's just so ugly," one of the girls said.

"You look like a maid," another girl said.

Their comments drained Helen's defiance, and she was back to who she had been before. Tears streamed down her cheeks as Margaret smiled triumphantly. The other girls snickered. Then a familiar voice rang out from behind Helen.

"Shut the hell up and leave my sister alone," Stella said.

The girls froze.

"I mean it. I'll get my friends over here if I need to," Stella said. "They won't like you pushing my little sister around."

Margaret's glare returned. She moved toward Helen. "Needed your big sister, huh? Can't take care of yourself?"

The words were barely out of her mouth when Stella burst forth, rushing past Helen until she was directly in front of Margaret. She struck the girl hard across the mouth. The other girls froze as Margaret howled. Stella grabbed Helen's hand, their mittens bright against the white playground and marched her off. Helen looked back once at those girls and then toward Stella whose face at that moment, flushed and determined, was the safest place she had ever known.

"I'm sorry," Stella said softly as they walked away. "I'm sorry."

From that day until Stella graduated high school, Helen and Stella went to and from school together, ate lunch together, and spent recess together. Helen was a small shadow of her sister, one that Stella's friends simply accepted without considering much. If anyone teased them, Stella's smart tongue shut it down, and eventually, no one said anything.

On the way home from school that day, Helen watched people disembark the El train at the Milwaukee and Fullerton stations and walk toward bright wooden houses with big windows. She imagined the lives inside those houses. She imagined parents who did not fight about money, about the length of skirt the mother wore, or about all the liquor in the house being gone. She imagined certainty; she imagined knowing. As a young girl walked toward one such house, Helen closed her eyes and felt her body move along with the girl's body, felt herself open the door of the girl's house and walk into a clean and sunny living room, the whole place filled with the faint smell of lilacs. A father sat in a recliner reading a newspaper, a golden retriever at his feet. The mother entered carrying a plate of cookies.

"How was your day, kitten?" she said. Her lipstick was perfect, her heels high and narrow.

Helen was just about to reach out for a cookie when a hand shook her shoulder.

"It's our stop," Stella said.

Helen's eyes opened to the sun shining through the train's dirty window, and they stood to exit the train. When the girls climbed the stairs of their building and walked through the door to their apartment that afternoon, their mother was on the phone with their Aunt Mavis.

"I better go, Mavis. My girls are home," she said. She threw her head back and laughed with her whole body. "I know. I know. My girls are two peas in a pod, just two peas in a pod," she said. "Nothing gets between my girls."

Chapter 3: The One Leaving

For Stella, the end of childhood could not come quickly enough. With each milestone she passed, a small fire of satisfaction ignited within her. She delighted in her body widening and rounding, in the thatches of hair thickening beneath her arms and between her legs. When she started menstruating, she smiled each time her uterus pained her. It was just another step on the path to exiting one world and entering another—a world she would design herself. After they moved from the city to Lisle, Stella stared out the window of her parents' small house and thought only of leaving. Her fantasies were elaborate; she imagined lying to get a job, hiding in stores after closing to sleep, and getting her own apartment. In these fantasies, Helen did not exist. But it was usually Helen—the sound of her, the sight of one of her possessions—that pulled Stella back into the present. Years ago, Stella had sworn she would watch over Helen for all their lives, but she told herself she had to leave home to go to college for them both. It was Stella's responsibility to venture out and explore the world for both of them so she could teach Helen what she had learned. And if she got out, she could get Helen out eventually, too. She would come back for Helen. That had never been a question.

On the day Stella moved to the dorms at the University of Wisconsin - Milwaukee, the weather unleashed all the hell it had on Lisle, Illinois. As Stella packed the last of her clothes, shoes, and toiletries, a late-summer storm rose. Her mother scurried around the little house, closing windows while her father drank a generous glass of bourbon—the cheap, high-octane stuff he swilled daily. After packing, Stella sat in the living room, watching the rain. Her father sat down, followed by her mother, and then Helen. The family was silent awhile as rain poured aslant hard enough that Mick, shooting the last of his bourbon and getting up for more, said, "I guess we're not going today."

Stella's mother fired a look at him. "We're going. Girls, we're going as soon as it lets up."

For a moment, the coalescence of the weather and the looming move trapped them all so that Stella felt like they were hanging together, paralyzed in some sort of ornamental globe.

"This might be the last time for a while that we're all together," her mother tried.

Stella nodded, but the spirit of the comment was so inane that she dug her fingernails into the dirty arm of the couch. At no point in recent memory had they spent happy time together as a family. That was not who they were. They spent holidays together, and for a few hours some semblance of familial sentiment emerged, but that ended either when

Stella's father was overserved or when her mother grew moody about an imperfection—the turkey too dry, the apples in the pie too hard. Outside of holidays, they did not regularly eat meals together; instead, they breezed in and out of the kitchen heating up whatever Frances had cooked that day. In the evenings, her parents gravitated to separate parts of the house if her father was home, and Stella took refuge in the bedroom she shared with her sister, avoiding the fallout of their parents' frequent fights.

Helen suddenly started laughing and soon laughed hard enough that she doubled over in her seat. Stella was not surprised. What their mom had said *was* funny.

"What's wrong with her?" Mick said, on the verge of hurt as usual. "What the hell is she laughing at?"

Stella, newly empowered by her eminent departure, looked at her father's face and joined her sister in laughter, unable to stop after starting.

"Don't give them any grief, Mick," Stella's mother said. "Leave them alone." She paused, stone-faced, and staring directly at Stella. "They're laughing because they're scared."

Stella's laughter slowed to a trickle. Helen had covered her face with her hands, but Stella could tell her laughter had given way to something else. Hands still across her face, she ran into the bathroom as the living room fell back into the sounds of rain and the occasional crash of ice into the side of Mick's glass.

The rain did let up, and soon they loaded Stella's things and left. On the drive to UWM, the car was mostly quiet as they sped alongside farmland teeming with corn, flat open spaces, gas stations, and country houses. The clouds parted, and the sky assumed a yellow shade of gray as pale sunlight appeared and disappeared, the road unfurling in front of the family. Once they reached campus, Stella quickly got out of the car and took her possessions from the trunk. Helen and her parents emerged slowly and stood in a line along the car. She faced them, her back to Purin Hall, the bland brick building about to become her home. Students ambled all around, endemic to the maze of buildings, grass, and trees.

"Let me walk you in," her mother said. She put her hands on Stella's shoulders and turned her toward the building. "Your dad and Helen can circle around, and I'll help you get settled."

"You don't——" Stella started to say but was interrupted by a slamming door. She snapped back around toward the car. Helen was no longer standing next to her father. "You don't have to," Stella finished, turning back toward her mother. "I can do it alone."

"Are you sure?"

"Yes. I should get in there."

Her mother hugged her first, and then her father, the alcohol stink of his breath spilling onto her. After hugging them, Stella knocked on Helen's car window. Helen's face flashed up, and Stella waved, but Helen looked back down at

her lap and resumed fingering a loose thread on the hem of
her dress.

Once in her room, Stella arranged her things, putting her
clothes in one of the cheap brown dressers that the room was
furnished with. She made her twin bed with a threadbare pair
of sheets from home and put her suitcase beneath it. She
realized she had nothing to hang on the walls——no pictures,
posters, or paintings. Her corner of the room was bare and
beige, unwritten. When she could think of nothing else to
do, she lay down in bed and stared up at the ceiling. Outside
the open window, the din of cars and people sounded. It was
the perfect soundtrack to this solitude, this freedom, which
was bliss. Then the wind blew, sending the smell of her
sheets, the smell of home, around the room. When she closed
her eyes, she imagined Helen alone in the back seat of their
parents' car. She imagined Helen sleeping alone in their
shared room. She imagined Helen alone enduring their
parents. She imagined Helen alone walking to school.

Only then did she begin to cry.

That first year, Stella learned she did not particularly like
college. She took a variety of classes that interested her but
had no clear connection to one another. The college
catalogue was a building of many apartments, small studios
in which she could live for a just awhile. Though she learned
a lot in those temporary quarters of art, science, and
psychology, she never found a place to stay. She could not

decide on a major or a career, and ultimately, she understood that she favored experience, especially in the spring when lazy breezes blew through open windows and the professors' voices drifted around her, never settling in her ears. All she wanted then was to drive around Lake Michigan in someone's car with the windows rolled down, smoke cigarettes, and turn the radio up.

On the weekends, when she wasn't checking at the A&P, she went to parties with girls she thought of as tolerable, which was the only word that fit them. They came from homes with pretty mothers who had jewelry boxes and fathers who drank only beer and never to excess, homes that were owned, not rented. While she was with these girls, she discovered her penchant for acting. She could pretend her real life away for long periods of time: her family's small, white rental house in Lisle growing, her mother's eyes never black and blue, her father's hands never shaking. She became skilled at deflecting questions about herself. Instead, she asked the girls about themselves, their lives, the boys they liked. The girls grew close to Stella. Several of them called her their best friend. But Stella would never have said that about them. To her, they were simply traveling companions with whom she drank, smoked, and made merry during her time in a foreign city, a foreign state. She called home once a week and told Helen about all she did. Helen listened passively, and even through the phone, Stella felt Helen's jealousy.

"I miss you, sister. And I won't be here forever," she often said before hanging up.

"Sure, OK," was Helen's usual response.

The only thing Stella truly enjoyed about college life was the boys. Away from everyone who knew her, she was novel, fresh. The boys stared at her when she walked into class. They stared at her when she crossed campus between classes, her brown hair billowing around her face like burnished armor. When they worked up the nerve, they invited her to movies, parties, study groups. They bought her lunches and dinners, poured her beers, lit her cigarettes. Though she talked and ate with several boys, only a few ever ended up in the back seat of a car or the back row of a movie theater with her. She was selective, and she bored easily. When they started with their protestations of love, she stopped seeing them as something to be conquered and rather as something ruined. Once that happened, they never looked the same, and she walked away. It hurt little to leave——a sweet and reminiscent pain——one she savored as she held close some trinket given to her by one of them.

By late April of that first year, several of the girls she had entrenched herself with decided not to live in the dorms the following year. Some planned to rent apartments and continue their studies, but the majority were dropping out to get married.

"It's why we go to college," one of the girls said as she packed. "I don't want to spend my life behind a desk or at a hospital. I want to be a mother."

Stella had a hard time understanding what was better about being a wife and mother than being behind a desk or helping sick people, but by that spring, she knew undoubtedly that college and the types of careers it offered were not for her either.

"What classes are you taking next?" her mother asked one night on the phone. "You must be planning for next year now."

"Yes," Stella said, as she wrote her name neatly in cursive over and over on the course catalog. "I have some really good ones picked out." She cleared her throat. She had never been good at lying to her mother.

"I'm so glad to hear that," her mother said. "I'm so happy for you. It's important for women to make their own way. I wish we could talk Helen into going. But I'm sure she won't go. I don't know what she'll do."

Stella let the line go quiet between them.

"Are you there?" her mother said.

Stella looped the J of her last name, Jenkot, right over the description of a British literature course.

"Yes, sorry, I'm still here."

"So you got an apartment for the summer? Are you subleasing from someone?"

"Yes, I found a place," Stella said.

"Good for you. That will work out perfectly. And Helen will be glad to have you back in Lisle again for a while."

Stella threw the catalog into the garbage.

"I'll be glad to get out of here," she said. That at least was not a lie. "Listen, I have to go. We'll talk soon, OK?"

When Stella hung up the phone, she pulled the lease agreement she had signed last week out of her desk drawer. She smiled and ran her fingers over where she had signed and dated the document.

Length of lease: 12 months, it said.

Chapter 4: The Chemist

Gerald Drozka had always been a chemist. His practice of science started when he was a child and his father gave him a chemistry set for Christmas one year. He wore the set out through various experiments, and when he finally exhausted it and broke several of its vials and beakers, his mother's kitchen became his new laboratory, her glass measuring cups his new glassware, her cupboards his stock of chemicals. He conducted his research with baking soda, vinegar, cornstarch, red cabbage, oil, and water. When he used the last of something for one of his experiments, his mother hounded him gently. "Waste not, want not," she said. Even though she admonished him, she never forced him to stop what he was doing, and secretly—Gerald realized when he was older—she had often bought a little extra of this or that specifically for him.

Throughout his education at Lake View High School on the north side of Chicago, he excelled in science courses, often spending time after school with his science teacher, Mr. Connelly, a black-haired, blue-eyed Irishman who had come to the United States as a teenager, who ate stew and soda bread for lunch, and who occasionally referred to his students as *lads*, correcting himself when the students snickered. Although some made fun of Mr. Connelly behind his back, Gerald never did. He could see that Mr. Connelly was a good man who, had he been well-born, probably wouldn't have become a teacher at all but rather a scientist. He spoke fondly of his college days, his eyes clouding whenever he recounted his professors and the equipment he had access to at the university. He encouraged Gerald not to stop college after just one degree in chemistry but to set himself on the long path.

"People are only going to become more and more educated. You've got to stay in school for as long as you can, Gerald. Go until there are no more degrees to be had in your field. You've got your whole life to work. There's no reason to rush into it if you don't have to," he said.

Gerald regarded this advice solemnly, and he didn't stop after finishing his bachelor's degree at the University of Chicago. He continued on to finish his master's degree ahead of schedule and then enrolled in the school's doctoral program.

It was while he was working on his doctorate that he met Stella. On an evening when a couple friends cajoled him to leave the city for a night out at their hometown bar, the Lisle Bowl, Stella sidled up to their table in the bar and said, "What are you having?" Her long brown hair was piled high on her head, and she wore red lipstick, a bead of which had settled on her slightly crooked front tooth. She had proud cheekbones and large, almond eyes that glittered in the alley bar's dim light. Tall and thin, she smelled like lilacs and cotton. As she spoke, the first thought Gerald had was that this was the woman he'd like to marry. Of course, the thought did not come to him like that; it wasn't even really a thought yet, but a feeling that would soon blossom into a thought. It was the feeling that he was losing something every time she walked away.

He went to the Lisle Bowl more frequently, despite its distance from the city, leaving if his Stella wasn't working. It took more than a month before she seemed to remember his face, but finally one day, she paused as she was taking the empty cans off his table and said, "You come in here a lot. What's your name?"

"Gerald," he stammered as his friends stared into their beers, smirking.

"Gerald. Jerry," she said.

No one called him Jerry. He had been Gerald his whole life, but somehow with her christening, he didn't mind it. It made him someone to her.

That night he lingered after his friends left, slapping him on the back unceremoniously as they walked out. Gerald was a little too tight, a little too absorbed by his desire, and without a ride home.

"She's going to drive me home," he had announced to his friends shortly before they left.

"Drozka, you're full of shit," his friend John said, reaching into his wallet and pulling out a card. "When she shoots you down, here's the number for a cab."

Gerald took the card and turned it in his hands before tucking it in his wallet and flashing John a middle finger. Then he waited for Stella to return. Amidst the music of pins and balls, cheers and curses, Gerald watched slow minutes on a large black rimmed clock tick by, taking the card out of his wallet and putting it in his shirt pocket after ten minutes. But then Stella appeared, and to his amazement, she settled in a chair across from him, put her legs up, and lit a cigarette.

"Where'd all the boys go?" she asked after her first drag.

"It was past their bedtime," he said.

"But not yours?"

Here she was, opening the door for him, and now he found himself reddening, his earlier confidence endangered by her cool. He sipped his beer and took a breath deep enough to taste her cigarette.

He shook his head. "No, not yet. I wanted to ask you something." He unearthed the nerve to look into her eyes, brown and gold, which sparkled in the dim light of the bar. "I wanted to ask you to give me a ride home."

"That's pretty bold."

He shrugged, bolstered by what he took to be a compliment. He was *bold*.

"Why should I give you a ride home?"

"Because you like me."

"I do?"

"Yes."

"What makes you think that?"

He took another sip of his beer.

"You touch my arm when you take my order. Every time."

Immediately after he said it, something changed in Stella; the power between them shifted.

She looked down, stubbed out her cigarette, and exhaled. "I'm done in an hour. Meet me out front," she said, standing up. She started walking away but then stopped and turned around. "And Jerry," she said, "maybe have a cup of coffee."

Gerald's face went hot, but then she winked and smiled.

He watched her walk across the room and start talking to one of the other waitresses who glanced furtively at Gerald over Stella's shoulder and smiled widely. Women were always doing things like that, he thought. And here he was, a smear on a slide being examined under their microscope. It didn't matter so much, he reasoned: she had agreed to take him home.

When her shift ended, they met outside as planned.

"Where to?" she asked.

"I live in Hyde Park."

"In the city?"

"In the city."

"OK," she said, shaking her head. She started the ignition and turned on the radio. It was an old country station, and Stella rolled down her window and lit a cigarette, singing along to Kitty Wells and Hank Williams. Gerald, feeling speech would simply ruin the moment, rolled down his window, closed his eyes, and listened to her sing.

The next thing he knew, she was saying his name softly and patting his arm. He awoke to see the city spreading before them and Stella started laughing.

"You need to tell me how to get to your place," she said.

"Damn it, oh shit, I'm sorry."

"It's OK," she said, laughing again.

"Are you going to ask me up?" she asked when they finally reached his apartment.

"Yes, of course," he said, happy she had made the move.

Once inside, they sat in his small, hot living room with a single desk fan blowing directly on them and drank whiskey on ice. They told one another short versions of how each had come to where they were. Their conversation meandered and flowed naturally; any silences were short, nearly unnoticed. Soon it was 4:00 a.m., and pink light was cracking the bottom of the sky. Stella stood to leave.

"I'll be seeing you again soon," she said.

"When?" he asked.

"Soon," she said, brushing his arm as she walked past him and out the door.

After he closed the door and went to pour himself another drink, he realized he hadn't asked her for her number. He opened the door and ran to the end of the hall, but she was gone. He cursed his ineptitude, drank his whiskey, and then walked to the bathroom to get ready for bed. There, on the shelf near the sink, was a small slip of paper with STELLA JENKOT printed neatly and below it, her number: 630-357-4244. He ran his fingers over the paper, feeling the indent of her hand.

Though it was 4:00 am, he was seized with joy and picked up the phone and dialed John, who answered, his voice thick with sleep.

"She gave me a ride home, asshole," Gerald said.

They only courted briefly before Gerald asked that she marry him. They were married in a small courthouse ceremony with Helen as the single bridesmaid. His parents were there; hers were not, though he never got a straight answer as to why they didn't attend. "We wanted to meet the parents," his mother lamented. Gerald held her off from saying anything to Stella. Bearing her own mother's absence had been enough for her, though he was sure Stella would never admit it. "She isn't her parents. Shame on them for not being here," his father said, clapping his shoulder.

In the second year after the wedding, Gerald made the decisions that would define their future. Like many other important occurrences in his life, the event which shaped the rest of his life happened at school. One of his professors was friends with an entrepreneur, Mr. Bradstreet, who was interested in starting a business that manufactured and sold industrial chemicals. Gerald's professor, a man he had never felt particularly close to, pinpointed him as a perfect candidate for the job. Mr. Bradstreet had the building and the money to buy the equipment, but what he needed was a chemist to set up and maintain the operation. Mr. Bradstreet was direct about what he wanted and what Gerald's responsibilities would be. The work would most likely be interesting at first, but it would quickly become rote. There would be little room for Gerald to experiment or develop anything new. What they would manufacture would be determined by the market. At first Gerald regarded the opportunity skeptically. He thought again of Mr. Connelly and his advice. *Don't stop, Gerald.* Taking the job meant leaving his PhD incomplete. He had never imagined himself as a company man; he had imagined he would find a job in academia, become tenured, publish his work. And though he wasn't particularly fond of teaching—the hordes of unfocused undergrads he'd have to endure—he thought it could provide Stella and him with a comfortable life. But a few days later, Mr. Bradstreet made him an offer, an offer much more generous than a university could ever give him.

As he considered what to do, he thought of Stella, his Stella, her beautiful brown-gold eyes. She was in her mid-twenties, just coming to the height of her beauty, and he knew she wanted a house in Lisle and a family. Already when they shopped, she would stop longingly in front of a little dress or a pair of corduroy pants and smile as she gently fingered the material. Then she would turn and look at him in the way she had when they had first started planning their life together.

"Isn't this sweet?" she would say, her voice high and light. "I think it's just so sweet."

He would smile and nod. "Yes," he would say, looking at her, not whatever it was she was touching. "Yes, it's perfect."

Although he knew that as a married man he should include his wife in his decisions, he only pondered what he thought she'd say instead of asking her. He did not know if he was afraid of what she'd say or if he was afraid of giving up what was left of his autonomy. *But it's my life,* he thought to himself when he was alone. *But it's our life,* he imagined her saying.

Though it hurt, he quit school and took the job, trading the unknown for the known. Once made, he did not regret his decision. He was able to buy the house in Lisle Stella had dreamed of. They would not want for any comfort. He was happy with the life he had chosen, but he could not deny that he missed science, the way he supposed an artist who stops making art misses even the sight of his brushes and paint, his clay and kiln. Or the way a writer who no longer writes must tell himself stories anyway. Most of the time, he was able to shrug this feeling off, but sometimes, he missed the lab so deeply—the rising action and then the climax of discovery, the precision, the beauty of possibility. When these feelings of loss came rushing to him as they did, always at night, he put a pillow over his head because even the slightest sound of air passing through Stella's nose or mouth would irritate him. When it was especially bad, he forced himself out of bed and downstairs.

In the kitchen, he baked. Since he was a chemist, the baking process was simple to him. It was ratio and reaction, and his kitchen—as it had been when he was a child—

became his lab. He baked dinner rolls, caramel rolls, baking powder biscuits. He made loaves of bread: wheat, white, rye, cinnamon raisin. And he did it all while Stella slept. Mornings after he baked, Stella walked down the stairs, her hair sleep shocked, the strap of her night gown hanging off her shoulder. Her eyes were moony and half-closed, and her smile was a dream.

"Bread," she would say, "you baked bread."

Chapter 5: The Drought

Men with their pawing hands, lurking eyes, and sharp teeth, men were not to be trusted. Men were wolves, big looming things that stalked and preyed. They saw others only in terms of purpose, the driving wheel of their actions. They were full of bluster and bravado that could turn to blows before anyone had the chance to put the word "stop" in the air. So, to Helen, men——men belonged in reserves of forest and prairie where they could be controlled and observed.

Helen had regarded each new man of Stella's as a threat because with each interloper, Helen faded to gray in her sister's eyes, becoming pixilated and thin, like a ghost. Intimacy was lost between the two of them in direct proportion to the growth of intimacy between Stella and her lovers. But thankfully, there was normally a ceiling to that intimacy: Stella's men never stayed too long. To Helen, the worst was that after Stella's dismissal, these men clung on awhile, driving past Helen and Stella's apartment, their wolfishness disarmed, their faces gaunt, juvenile.

Gerald had been different right away. Stella was actually worried Gerald wouldn't call or Gerald would grow tired of her. Helen had never seen Stella change her clothes or her hair as much as she did for Gerald. So she settled in as though waiting for a storm to bear down on her, for already she knew he was there to stay. Now it would always be the three of them, sisterly secrets saved for the rare occasions when Gerald was absent. Forced to accept him, Helen regarded him coolly and formally, as she treated almost everyone except Stella. But, in the ardor and anxiety of his courtship of Stella, Helen could sense that Gerald longed to please her as well as her sister. He treated her with a gentleness to which she was not accustomed and seemed genuinely affronted when she was aloof.

She was not surprised when one morning he appeared at the apartment while Stella was working. Still she treated him incredulously as he stood on the front stoop, wearing his Sunday best—he was always wearing his Sunday best—and holding a loaf of bread.

"Stella's not here," she said.

"I know. I dropped by to say hi to you."

"OK," she said flatly.

"I brought this for you," he said, thrusting the loaf toward her like a child embarrassed of his own gift.

"What is it?"

"Cinnamon raisin. I made it this morning. Thought I'd drop it off for you to have for breakfast."

"A little late for breakfast."

He looked down at his shoes.

"I mean, I already ate," Helen said. As she said it, she felt herself softening against him, which made her angry. "I can't eat breakfast twice."

"Jesus, Helen, it's a gesture."

Helen read the defeat in his eyes, and she wanted it to please her, but it didn't. Instead, she felt guilty.

"I don't know what I'll do with a whole loaf of this."

"You'll eat some. You'll share some with your sister. You'll put some in the freezer if you need to. Here——take it."

"Fine," she said, taking the bread from him savagely. "Thanks."

She turned without another word and shut the door, leaning against it, her heart beating quickly; she knew she had behaved badly, and Stella was sure to hear about it. She ran her tongue across her crooked teeth and then moved her lips back and forth over them, letting the points of her incisors dig in. Sometimes she thought she would be better at all this——at being a sister, a friend, a human being——if only she had been born with straight, white teeth.

As she often did when she was ashamed, she thought of her grandfather. It was his hands she always saw. Because he was a particular type of man, he had a particular type of hands. His fingers were long and thin, the nails extending farther past his fingertips than they should. Frequently, he applied a thick, yellow crème that smelled of butter, so his skin was always soft and nearly damp. His were the hands of a man who didn't like to get dirty, a man who had made his living wearing suits and selling encyclopedias door to door.

Every day of his adult working life, he had been received in the homes of families. Wives shook his hands and drank his flattery. Children laughed at his jokes and ate the butterscotch candies he gave them. With the length of his fingernails, he was able to flip through the fine pages of the sample volumes he showed his customers.

"These books will tell you everything you need to know from Aardvark to Zygote," he said at the end of a pitch.

"You must know so much," a housewife replied, touching her hair gently.

He leaned into her, close enough so he was sure she could smell his aftershave, a knockoff of some expensive brand.

"I've got an encyclopedic mind," he winked.

"Oh stop," the housewife said, her pulse quickening a little as she glanced nervously at her front door, praying her husband did not come home early.

At least that is how Helen imagined his days must have been, full of opportunities and flirtations, full of games meant to mimic something like life.

Helen's memory was arranged emphatically, and because she had purposefully forgotten lesser memories, she now had only one memory of him. She had thought of it regularly for the last 15 years. She thought of it especially when she was staring down at her grandfather's hands, the nails clipped uncharacteristically short, as they rested on his chest and his body rested in an oak casket. During that recollection of this particular moment, she was happy. She smiled at his body, stifling a fit of laughter, which she quickly disguised as a sob when Stella nudged her sharply with an elbow.

In that one clear recollection of her grandfather, Helen was wearing a white dress. She was 10 years old, and this is what she remembered:

Midwestern heat and humidity. A picnic in the postage-stamp sized backyard of her Aunt Mavis's house. The grandfather, her father's father, patting his forehead with a handkerchief. Her father laughing, already into the bourbon further than he needed to be. Her mother rolling her eyes. Her sister running around with the tall, handsome cousin everyone loved. Her grandmother stationed under the shade of the only tree in the backyard. Sweat rolling down everyone's glasses as they sipped beer or lemonade or water. Smoke rising from the old black grill. A merciful breeze every so often.

Then she remembered looking down and seeing her lemonade glass empty. She felt a pain in the low place of her belly. She crossed one leg over the other while sitting in the grass, but it didn't go away, so she got up and walked into the cool, empty house to relieve herself. It was dark inside because her aunt had drawn the shades to keep the heat out, and the only sound was the radio, news radio, playing a story about farmers and drought. The farmers were talking about their crops and how there wasn't going to be enough corn for them to sell, no, there wasn't going to be enough corn, and if there wasn't enough corn, there wouldn't be enough feed, and if there wasn't enough feed, there wouldn't be enough meat. Prices would skyrocket. People would go hungry.

She heard it as she turned on the light to the bathroom, as she closed the door, and as hot urine flowed from her, relieving the pain in her belly. Suddenly, almost simultaneously with the relief, the door to the bathroom opened. Then he was in the doorway, his thin hands with their too long fingernails at his side.

"I'm going!" she said to him, but he did not move. Instead, he walked in and shut the door behind him.

She tried to make herself stop, but she couldn't stop. It just kept coming and coming, and then she realized it didn't matter anyway because he was in front of the door, a barrier between her and all means of escape. She pushed and pushed, trying to make it all come out quickly so she could stand and cover herself.

Finally, she was done, and she pulled up her underwear, the ones with the days of the week printed on them, this pair *Saturday,* without even wiping. A single drop of urine flowed down her thigh as she stood, her skirt falling around her.

"Don't forget to wash your hands now," he said.

She walked to the sink, and then he was behind her. Putting his arms around her waist and holding her up so that her hands were in the sink, he rubbed himself against her, over and over. The water grew scalding hot, and she watched her hands turn red but did not move them.

She was washing her hands. That was all. It was taking a long time.

Then suddenly, he grunted and stopped, releasing her.

"Don't you say a damn word," he said, pulling her to face him. "Not even a peep, little mouse." He let her shoulders go. "Now get out," he snarled. "Get out of here."

It was the first time she heard this tone in his voice; it would not be the last.

She flew towards the door and ran back into the hot sun where everyone was still drinking and eating and laughing and playing. Somehow she felt older, as though a very long time had passed, and she was the only one who knew it. She cursed all of them, each and every one who never had to venture into the sepulchral depths of the house and be trapped by him. She did not want to speak or look at any one of them, so she found a spot in the corner of the yard where a neighbor's tree provided only enough shade to cover her small body and waited for her grandfather to emerge. After a few minutes he did, wearing different pants, walking right over to her father, taking a beer out of the cooler.

"Hear the latest about the drought?" he asked.

Chapter 6: The Postman, The Wife, The Servant

Stella had never been jealous. Jealousy meant giving up power. Besides, she never allowed cause to be jealous. She was the type of woman who exacted exclusive devotion, and if not given precisely what she wanted, she walked away. Even when she found the letters from Sarah buried beneath some magazines in Gerald's nightstand drawer, she did not feel jealous. She looked at them clinically, as though they were a problem to be solved. The problem dictated that she began reading them and so she did with the detached curiosity one exercises while reading history books. But this wasn't history, nor was it the past. The most recent letter had arrived only last week, addressed to Gerald's office. She read it first:

Last night was the dream I have most. The big one. The one I can't get rid of. It doesn't matter what I do before bed. I leave on the TV or the radio or I read those romance books, the ones you always said would rot my brain. It doesn't matter how much I try to fill up with all the happiness in the world, I still have the dream. Then it takes me half the day to shake it. You know how that it is, don't you Gerald? You know how long it can take to get rid of the dream feeling even when you try to load up your mind in the morning? I try to load up my mind in the morning, but I still feel like I'm in the dream, like I'm right in the middle of the dream. Like it just got through happening to me.

Anyway, so in the dream, we're all there. Me and you and Freddy and Tom. Jenny and Mary. The whole gang all together again. I can't figure out where we are though. Somewhere that looks familiar, but there's nothing really telling enough for me to know for sure. We're laughing about something. Everybody. You remember the way we all used to make fun of Jenny for that damn idiot laugh? Well, she's doing that. Tommy's poking at her. And everyone is just so happy. That's the first part of the dream. Happy, happy. Then Jenny and Tommy get up and say they're going to go out for a smoke. Freddy and Mary go, too. So it's just me and you. I stand up to go sit at the other side of the table. That's when it starts hurting, really hurting. Like a knife in my belly. And I look down. Then I see the blood. Not a lot. One drop, then another, then another on the ground between my feet. It's like my heartbeat. Every time my heart beats, it hurts and bleeds. I can't move. So, I just stand there. I look up and I see everyone outside smoking and laughing. Then I turn around, but you're gone because you're out there, too. Everyone is out there, and I'm standing inside just looking at the blood. And I'm so scared, but it doesn't matter because my mouth won't work and besides, there's no one to hear me anyway.

When I wake up, my heart's always beating really fast. I check all around me to make sure there's no blood. I touch the bed and the pillows and blankets. But there isn't any. There never is, of course. It's funny, isn't it? Isn't it funny what you can do to yourself while you're sleeping?

The letter ended right there, signed *Love, Sarah.* She set it down and then picked up the phone and dialed the bank where she worked as a teller.

"Hal, it's Stella. I'm not feeling well...Everything is fine...but no, I'm not coming in at all...Ask Jeannie. I covered her shifts before. She owes me."

After hanging up, she made a fresh pot of coffee and sat at the kitchen table, reading the other letters voraciously. She tore through them as though she were reading someone's diary, as though the story of another person was forming and filling and growing heavy inside of her and soon it was impossible to know where the person in the letters ended and where Stella began. For a while she forgot to check the dates on them as she read, but when she stopped, demarcating the space where the letters ended and she began, she focused only on the dates. *How long had these letters been coming? How frequently? Were any of the dates special?* She ran her fingertips over and over the alphanumeric markers of time, feeling the sad imprint of the other woman's hand. Dates were empirical evidence. Dates did not lie.

After reading them all, she carefully rebound the letters and put them back in his drawer. She thought about calling someone, Helen perhaps, but she was not ready. Saying everything aloud would make it true. Instead, she walked to the corner store and bought a pack of cigarettes. She chain-smoked all the way home. As her body twitched with nicotine and an ache formed in her head, she was proud of the minor betrayal she had just committed. Gerald hated it when she smoked.

That evening, she waited like a nervous teenager for Gerald to come home. Each action she engaged in was momentous. She brushed her teeth, refreshed her makeup, and touched up her hair, trying to remember she had power. Silence was her power. There were hinges, she knew, and once one wrong thing was said, the hinges bent, and people went from being parallel to being perpendicular. Saying nothing would give her the upper hand. Finalizing the details of the artifice she would present to Gerald, she smiled at herself and practiced saying hello in a way that would sound natural and——more importantly——neutral. She put on a clean dress, one he liked. She imagined that once he came home and they resumed their routine, she would feel better. Love was not the grace of marriage. Routine was. And she knew routine would always have and hold and keep them for as long as they both should live, despite whoever appeared in the periphery.

But as they sat quietly over dinner, Stella kept imagining Sarah at the table with them. She imagined what Sarah would wear, what she would say, what she would eat. It was hard work, all this imagining.

"Are you OK?" Gerald asked.

Stella realized she had been rolling a chunk of his homemade wheat bread back and forth between her fingertips and staring off.

"Fine," she said, dropping the bread on her plate. "I'm just tired."

"I'll do the dishes. You go relax," he said, smiling and touching her hand.

As his skin breathed into hers, she wondered if he had ever imagined her finding the letters. She wondered what his defense would be. Above all she wondered if he and Sarah had clandestine meetings, lips brushing cheeks on the El train in some deep part of the city, a part Stella had never traveled to her whole life, a part Gerald and Sarah knew only in tandem, entire tomes of definition arising from concrete and stone. But she said nothing because if it were true, she did not want to know, not really. Knowing would only mean change, and change meant losing something. There was nothing she wanted to lose now.

The next morning, she woke before sunrise, the reality of the previous day's findings waking with her, her heart pounding with it. She was tempted to make a scene. She was tempted to grab the letters and throw them at Gerald. She was tempted to scream and claw and fight. But instead, remembering the power she had in silence, she feigned sleep until after Gerald showered, dressed, and went downstairs. Then she got out of bed and sat at the kitchen table while he ate his breakfast. He kissed her on the cheek as he always did before he left.

When he was gone, she pulled the letters from the drawer and checked the return address. Sarah lived across town. For a second Stella entertained the thought of going to Sarah's house, but that would be letting jealousy take over. Besides, what would she say if she did show up at the woman's front door? Instead, she combed the letters for any mention of where Sarah worked. She thought one of the more monotonous letters had said something about it. Finally, the mention appeared. Sarah worked at a salon. *Of course, a beautician,* Stella thought. They were a breed of women Stella loathed. Their careers involved superficiality and immediate gratification. They gossiped like packs of useless hens, caged and clawing at each other's feathers. Sarah's henhouse was a salon called Moxie, and Stella knew exactly where it was.

She glanced at herself in the mirror; today was as good a day as any to have her hair done. It was only a little thing, wasn't it? She would not make a scene; she would simply investigate.

The salon was housed in a timid concrete building perched on the end of a block just off Maple Avenue. An aging blue sign hung like a stiff flag from the side of the building. Stella parked her car in its little lot, lingering over a cigarette before walking in. Her hands trembled; she was nauseous as though either her stomach might contract or her bowels might void at any given second. She fought through the sickness and forced herself into the salon.

The inside of the place matched the humble nature of the outside. It had three stations on each wall and a counter at the front. Natural light flooded in, which briefly disguised the fact that one of the fluorescent lights was flickering. In two of the chairs sat women with curlers in their hair. Quietly, they flipped through magazines, glancing up at Stella upon hearing the door open. The woman at the front desk smiled brightly as Stella approached.

"Hi there. Do you have an appointment today?"

"No, I was hoping maybe you could fit me in."

The receptionist furrowed her brow, looking down at the appointment book.

"I just need a trim," Stella said.

"Do you normally see someone here?"

Stella hesitated for a second. "Sarah."

"Sarah?"

"Yes, well, I mean a friend recommended her to me."

"Great! She has an opening in about an hour. I just need your name.

"Stella."

"Would you like to wait here or come back?"

Stella briefly considered the woman's question, but she knew the answer.

"I'll wait here."

If she left, she might change her mind.

"Sounds good. There are plenty of magazines over there, and I can get you a cup of coffee if you'd like. Would you like a cup of coffee?"

"Sure—thanks."

The woman took Stella's coat. As Stella sat down in one of the vinyl-covered chairs, she realized that her cigarettes were in the jacket pocket, a fact which would make the wait even longer. The receptionist returned with her coffee, and Stella sipped it, absently flipping through the glossy pages of an old *Good Housekeeping*. Something occasionally grabbed her attention—a hairstyle, a dress, an advertisement. Mostly she looked at each page multiple times, struggling to keep her mind still for long enough to digest what was on it.

From the back of salon, she heard laughter, and when she looked up, she saw a woman she instinctively knew to be Sarah. The woman appeared slightly older, which made sense since Gerald was also a couple years older. She was tall and thin with pale skin and fine, red brown hair. Her nose was small and pointed, and though Stella did not think the woman more attractive than she, Stella could understand why a man would like her. She had a conversational beauty, a loveliness that emerged as she talked and smiled.

Realizing she was staring, Stella refocused on a page in her magazine until Sarah's voice interrupted her.

"Are you Stella?" the woman asked.

"Yes, yes I am."

"Nice to meet you. I'm Sarah."

Sarah reached out and Stella took her hand. It was cool and dry, rougher than she had expected.

"I just wanted to stop over and say hi while my other client's hair is setting. So, what are we doing to your hair today? Just a cut?"

"Yes—a trim, really."

"Well, I think I can handle that," Sarah said, smiling so genuinely and warmly that Stella almost felt guilty for being there in the first place. She walked back to her station, and Stella continued trying to read her magazine, but the rest of the wait passed quickly, and soon she was in Sarah's care.

Before Sarah started making any of the small talk that hairdressers did so skillfully, she led Stella to the chair where clients' hair was washed. She turned on the water, and Stella barely heard her voice over its rush.

"Is this too hot?" she asked.

"No."

Stella closed her eyes as Sarah gently began rubbing floral-scented shampoo in her hair, her fingertips massaging every inch of Stella's scalp. She was gentle but firm, and she hummed as she worked. Stella thought of Gerald then; somehow she could feel his presence, all three of them twisted up together. The thought gave her pain, and she wanted to leap out of the chair and run to her car, but then Sarah turned off the water.

"Meet me in the chair over there," she said.

Obediently, Stella walked to the chair and sat down, thinking of what she wanted to say. She thought of asking Sarah outright if she was sleeping with Gerald, but it seemed uncouth to be so forthright. She did, however, want to know if what she thought was happening was indeed happening.

"So, we're just trimming the ends today?"

"Yes," Stella replied. She was busy staring at her own reflection in the mirror while also studying Sarah's. They looked very different——the shapes of their faces, the height of their cheekbones, the way their lips moved when they spoke. It was strange to know Gerald had loved them both. Their eyes met in the mirror as Sarah ran her hands through Stella's hair.

"About a half inch?"

"Sure."

"All right, I can do that for you," she said, combing through Stella's wet hair. "Having a good day?"

"Yeah, how about you?"

"A little tired, but good."

"Didn't sleep well?"

"No. I am not a good sleeper. Ever since I was little it's been that way."

"I completely understand. I'm that way, too."

"Yeah?" Sarah pinned up sections of Stella's hair and began to cut the bottom most layer.

"I dream a lot. And my dreams wake me up," Stella said. Her heart pounded with the knowledge of what she was doing.

"I know what you mean. I have these really vivid dreams all the time."

"The ones that have a way of sticking with you all day. You try to distract yourself, but you just can't shake them."

Sarah stopped cutting and stepped in front of her. "It's awful, isn't it?"

"It really is."

"I have this same one over and over. You ever have recurring ones?" Sarah asked as she resumed cutting.

Stella knew precisely what dream Sarah was talking about.

"Sometimes. What is yours?" she asked.

"It's not going to sound like much."

"That's OK. I'm interested in dreams."

"No, really, you don't want to hear it. It's a little disturbing."

"I've got a strong stomach."

Sarah's scissors paused.

"Seriously," Stella pushed, "I'm very interested in dreams, and I know a lot about them. Maybe I can help you figure out what it means."

"I don't know if I believe in all that."

The scissors began moving again.

"Try me. I might make you into a believer."

"Really, I——"

"Are you scared of something?" Stella asked. She saw her own eyes turn vicious, flat in the mirror.

"Not scared, of course," she said.

Stella said nothing, using silence as her tool once again.

Finally, Sarah began to speak. "Well, in the dream, I'm with people I know from college. My old group of friends. My college boyfriend is there, too. We're all just sitting around a table. Everyone's laughing. I hear my friend laughing. She had this laugh you really could recognize, you know? And then they were all outside and I was the only one inside, but I could see them through the window." She paused. "I don't know——it gets strange from here."

"They always do," Stella said.

The scissors stopped again, just behind Stella's ear.

"Anyway, all of a sudden, my stomach starts to hurt. It feels like someone is stabbing me, the worst pain you can imagine. I kind of lean over and hold my stomach and then I see it." Sarah's eyes met Stella's in the mirror. "I see blood on the ground."

"You're bleeding in the dream?"

"I just see drops of blood on the floor. Not a lot of blood, but in the dream I know there's going to be more blood. I can tell something bad is going to happen."

The scissors resumed, snapping shut on a layer of Stella's wet hair.

"What do you think it means?" she asked.

"I thought that's what you were going to tell me," Sarah said.

The scissors paused briefly.

Stella struggled to think quickly of an offering, any offering to get Sarah to continue. As seconds ticked past, she realized an offering didn't have to be true. It was a means to get the truth from someone else.

"My mom used to have this same dream over and over again. It was a nurse putting a stillborn baby in her arms. She'd wake up sweating and shaking and my dad would have to comfort her and talk to her until she relaxed. When I was older, she told me she had a miscarriage right before I was born. And she figured that was why she kept having the dream. She could understand why it was happening, but that didn't make it any less awful."

The story tumbled from her tongue easily. It was pure fiction, but Stella was sure it would work. Sarah, after all, was a hairdresser. Confession was a key part of her profession.

Sarah walked in front of her and leaned back against the counter. Her eyes were wide, her lower lip nearly atremble. "Really?" she said.

"Yes, it was awful," Stella said, and at that moment, she really felt that it *had* been awful. It was easy to believe her own lie. She looked Sarah dead in the eyes, mirroring the woman's pain.

"Because that's what happened to me."

"A miscarriage?"

Sarah nodded. She returned to cutting, the scissors eating at Stella's ends. "It was a long time ago. I was in college when I got pregnant. My college boyfriend was the father, and we——"

"What was his name?" Stella blurted out.

The scissors paused, and Sarah looked at her curiously in the mirror.

"Gerald. Why?"

Stella's hands went numb. The cape she wore started to choke her, and again she wanted to run. "Just curious," she said.

"Anyway, it was a long time ago." Sarah resumed cutting.

"I'm sorry—I interrupted you—finish what you were saying."

"There isn't much to say, I suppose. We were going to get married. And then I lost the baby. Neither one of us could save the other." She was quiet for a moment. "I guess that's the way it goes," she said finally, swallowing the last word as the scissors bit off more of Stella's hair.

It all made sense now. Stella knew from this woman's sadness that Gerald could not be sleeping with her nor would he want to. But she was still angry, for he and this woman had shared a child. A child was a child, even if it was no longer alive. And a child was something she hadn't yet shared with Gerald.

"What happened to him?" Stella asked.

The scissors paused.

"Are you still in contact with him? Is he married?"

"I don't know," Sarah said. "I don't really know."

The women were silent as Sarah's scissors continued. Stella had nothing else to say. She had learned what she came here to learn. Right now she did not know if she felt better or worse. She did not know if she would tell Gerald—or anyone else—what she knew. In the near future, however, she would pretend like everything was normal, like nothing had changed.

But as she watched the reflection of her husband's ex-lover in the mirror, she realized there was only one way to fix all of this: she needed to get pregnant.

Chapter 7: Dolls

Despite the way she felt about men, Helen had wanted nothing more her whole life than to have a baby. Growing up, she collected dolls as practice for motherhood. Most of them were secondhand, their plastic arms scratched, their eyes prone to malfunction, their clothes moth-bitten and worn. She brought them home from garage sales or thrift stores, and many times, knowing her affection for dolls, people gifted them to her. She loved every one and treated each with the same care a mother would have a real infant.

Throughout her girlhood, the dolls nested in dresser drawers or took turns slumbering in a small wooden cradle. Although she thought the dolls slept when she slept, sometimes she woke in the night to faint cries and followed the sound to her babies, trying to discern which was in distress. She touched each doll's forehead to check its temperature and slipped her hand between each doll's legs to feel whether it had soiled its diaper. The process of identifying the sad doll could be arduous. Some nights she made her decision arbitrarily or chose the newest in the collection to soothe. She would pick it up and say, "Hush," while patting its back rhythmically until something in both the doll and her quieted. If after that ritual neither she nor the doll could sleep, she whispered nursery rhymes into its ear as her mother had done for her.

There was a little girl,
Who had a little curl,
Right in the middle of her forehead.

And when she was good,
She was very, very good.
But when she was bad, she was horrid!

Then, on lucky nights, both she and the doll were pulled quickly to sleep. Sometimes, however, the doll could not be soothed, and she would have to hold it so tight against her body that its plastic limbs left marks on her skin. On those nights her sleep was shallow, and if the doll fell out of her grasp, she would wake with a cantering heart and reach for it as mothers reach for their newborns to make sure they are still breathing. Those nights always came at the worst possible times: when she had a test the next day, when her parents were fighting, when the house felt off-kilter, the foundation shifting beneath her.

She kept up her habit of the dolls in secret long after girls her age had given them up. At 14, when she started menstruating, she finally relented and put all her babies in the attic. After, she fantasized about finding abandoned children, about infants left in baskets where only she would stumble upon them, about immaculate conception, virgin birth. When her longing for a baby was at its peak—especially when Stella was out past curfew or when her parents' fighting was particularly brutal—she heard babies crying, and she would open the attic door with trepidation and switch on the single bare bulb that lit the room. She would find the box labeled *Helen Dolls* and open it to see her discarded children in various states of dress and disrepair. Innocent babes who had suffered through untempered heat and cold. Innocent babes who in their abandonment cried for her. She would pick them up one by one and comfort each, running her fingers through their coarse hair, taking in their plastic and rubber effluvia. When she could no longer hear the crying, she methodically put them back in the box and returned to bed where she slept in fits of dream.

Once she and Stella grew into women, the dream of having a child drifted further from Helen but not Stella. Stella was the lucky sister. Stella had Gerald. Soon, certainly it would be soon, Helen knew, Stella would get pregnant, leaving her behind yet again. The whole business made Helen melancholy, desperate.

One Thursday afternoon, Helen went downtown to shop for Christmas presents at Macy's on Michigan Avenue. As she walked past the men's shoe department, she saw a boy no more than two years old, tottering through the displays. He had brown curly hair, rosy cheeks, and he wore a cheap-looking winter coat, handmade mittens hanging from strings at the sleeves. He picked up one men's dress shoe, shook it in his tiny hand, and then placed it haphazardly back on the shelf. Pretending to look at a rack of suits, she watched him toddle through the shoes and then cross the aisle, dodging the legs of adults who looked down and smiled. He meandered through dress shirts, slacks, sport coats. She waited for his mother, his father, his auntie, for someone to claim him, but more time went by and no one came. Finally, the boy realized he was alone. Then it began, a familiar noise, the whimper just before the cry of a child. A spasm passed through the middle of her body, and she closed her eyes for a second, remembering that sound from when she was much younger; it was the sound her dolls had made from their cribs and the attic. What had happened to her dolls after she moved out? She had looked back at the box once before leaving. *Can I just leave this here?* she asked her mother. *Of course, honey,* her mother said, even though her mother was already planning to leave Helen's father. Helen couldn't have known that in six months her mother would be in a low-rent apartment above a laundromat, living only with what she had been able to pilfer from the house. By then, it was too late to go back for the dolls, but she had never forgotten about them or ceased feeling guilty for abandoning them.

The little boy's whimper grew into a wail, and she knew the only thing that could stop it was to hold the boy and calm him, as she had done so often with her dolls. Without another thought, she walked over and scooped him up in her arms. He immediately fussed, but she pulled a chocolate out of her purse and gave it to him, distracting and quieting him momentarily.

"Where's your mom?" she asked.

"Mama?" he said, a small drop of saliva teetering on his lower lip.

"Is she here?"

"Mama," he said, putting the chocolate in his mouth.

"Where is your mama?"

"Mama," he said again, this time pointing a chubby finger off toward the women's dressing rooms.

"Is your mama over there?" Helen asked, pointing in the same direction.

"Mama," he said, looking down and putting his hands together.

Helen held him tightly as he squirmed and walked toward the dressing room. She waited for a moment until the saleswoman's back was turned and then walked in with the boy.

"Is your mama here?" she asked, putting him down on his feet and stepping back from him.

The boy looked around and began to wail anew.

"No, shhh...don't...shhh," she said, kneeling. His whole face was red with misery.

"Everything OK?" the saleswoman, suddenly behind her, asked.

"I'm sorry——he just wandered in here, and he's overtired," Helen said with the authority of a parent. It felt good to stand in, to claim him as her own.

"Oh, poor little guy. Be a good boy for your mom, OK buddy?" the saleswoman said. "Do you want a piece of candy?"

The clouds on the boy's face drifted as he stared at the saleswoman.

"Candy?" the saleswoman said, pulling a mint out of her pocket.

The boy took the candy.

"What's your name?" she asked.

"Can you tell the nice lady your name?" Helen said.

The boy merely looked from her face to the saleswoman's face and then back again.

"What's your name?" the saleswoman repeated.

Still the boy said nothing, so Helen scooped him up, which only made him cry again.

"Bobby," Helen blurted out. "It's Bobby. I have to get him home for his nap," she said. "Thanks for the candy."

"Sure," the saleswoman said. "Get that little one home."

Helen rushed out of the dressing room, afraid to be caught in her lie with the saleswoman looking on. Once outside the dressing room with the boy in her arms, she did not know where to turn, for at any turn, the boy's mother or father or sister or brother might lurk, shattering Helen's dream of having him as her own. She had to get out of the store as quickly and quietly as possible.

Near the fragrance, she put her hand on the side of his head so that his face was obscured as he continued crying.

The girls at the counter smiled sympathetically. Of course, they didn't know who Helen was, who the boy was. The word *kidnap* rang in Helen's mind as she neared the door. *Kidnap?* No, not *kidnap*. That was what someone else might call it but not what it really was. Kidnapping was a term assigned to a variety of situations, some of which could be justified once put into context. Like this one. This little boy had no one and she saw him and he needed her.

When they finally reached the street, she put the boy on his feet, and they started walking away from Michigan Avenue down East Pearson Street where there was slightly less foot traffic. The boy was still upset, but he had stopped crying. She wondered if his allegiance was changing as it could so quickly in children of his age. She stopped and pulled him into the doorway of a closed shop.

"Stay here," she said, and then walked backward a few paces. It only took three steps before he started sobbing again. She returned to him, picked him up, and held him tightly against her chest. "It's all right," she said. "It's all right, baby." In the warm confines of her embrace, his howl hushed. She set him down and tested him one more time before she was satisfied, before she could fully feel the shift in him.

She stood there in the tiny alcove holding the boy until he fell asleep and her arms grew tired. At least half an hour had passed. She imagined police would soon flood the store looking for him. That didn't give her much time to make the decision: either she took him far away and did it now or she found a way to take him back inside the store. As she held the sleeping boy, she was grateful for this time alone with him. She had comforted; she had consoled, and so, yes, for these halcyon moments, she had been a mother. "I should have been your mother," she whispered to the boy. "I would have been a good mother to you," she said.

With that, it was time to take the boy back to where someone would find him.

She walked toward Macy's and leaned around the corner, seeing a squad car out front. That entrance surely wouldn't do, so she found a different, smaller entrance on the other side. It opened to the girls' section. While that section's saleswoman helped a mother and daughter, Helen ducked into the dressing room with the boy. She went into the largest stall and laid him down on the small bench in the corner. His eyes flickered open and then closed. "Shhh," she said, "It's all right." She watched him for a moment, the child she should have had, and then rushed out of the store as he waited for someone to come forth and carry him home.

Chapter 8: A Day Off

On his days off, the Mortician stayed in public as much as possible. He walked through shopping malls, ate in restaurants, drank in bars, and rode El trains as far as they would take him. It felt good to be surrounded by the noise and stink and business of life. He was lonely most of the time, and when he wasn't working, he did not want to think of sadness and loss, so he kept near the living.

Strangers may have thought he was a doctor, a lawyer, a real estate agent. He dressed and spoke well and carried himself with the type of dignity befitting any number of professional careers. He was not ashamed of what he did for a living; he knew he performed a valuable service and did it well. But there was a stigma around his profession. Death had been taken out of houses. It had been cleaned and shined and euphemized beyond recognition. People were more scared of death now than ever before, all part of the great American undying. He was not afraid. He thought all people owed it to themselves to spend a little time with the dead.

His first experience with the dead had come when he was just a few months shy from graduating high school. His mother had left his father and him years before for another man, a man who had taken her north to Superior, Wisconsin, to live in a cabin on Lake Superior. After she left, the Mortician thought about her every day, and more on days when the letters he sent her were returned. Above all, he wondered if she was happy. He kept these thoughts to himself though, for any time he mentioned her, he could see his father's whole body tense up and his face redden. Whether it was with anger or grief, the Mortician would never know, but his father didn't let it destroy them. They simply soldiered on, taking turns cooking meals and cleaning the house. They lived as well as they could, and each would have said he was happy.

But spaces of contentment seldom last long, and when the Mortician was on the precipice of becoming a man, the terrain of his world irrevocably shifted. One ordinary Wednesday morning, he called his father for breakfast, but his father did not appear. Curious, the Mortician went into his room and found him lying there pale and cold, the disheveled blankets on the bed the only clue of unrest. Standing alone with the morning sun rising, a breeze blowing the thin blue curtains in and out, in and out, he missed his mother more than he ever had, for he didn't know what to do next. Someone else was supposed to be there to help. Someone else was supposed to make the arrangements. Someone else was supposed to take care of his father's affairs. Overwhelmed, he sat in the wooden chair across the room from the bed and watched the sun come up higher and higher until its light was directly in his face and he had to close his eyes. When he closed his eyes, he heard something like a sigh, and he snapped them open and turned toward where his father lay.

"What's that, Pop?" he said. Then he shook it off, feeling silly for even having thought he heard anything at all. He turned back to the sun, but as soon as he did, he heard a similar sound——this time, however, he swore he heard the man say *Go*. "You want me to go, Pop?" he said, but there was no response. Still, he felt something, as though his father were now inside him, as though he had become both his father and himself, and he had to carry on conversations between them.

Call the ambulance first, his father said. *You know what funeral home. Same one that took care of your granddad. No use sitting around wishing. Wish in one hand, shit in the other and see which one fills up first.* His father laughed.

"Got it, Pop," he said.

I love you.

"I love you, too. You can count on me, Pop." He said "Pop" over and over, feeling a power in the word.

This was when he learned it was possible to talk to the dead. All one had to do was say their names.

At the Clark Family Funeral Home, he expected to be greeted by an ashen-faced man with dark circles under his eyes and a black suit. But instead he was greeted by Mr. Clark, a younger man——likely in his late 30s——with tan skin who wore a charcoal-colored suit. A woman, presumably his wife, was also there, her wavy strawberry-blonde hair catching the light from a large window behind Mr. Clark's desk. As soon as he walked in the room, the woman beckoned him to sit down and put a cup of coffee in his hand.

"Tell me about your dad," Mrs. Clark said.

Mr. Clark smiled.

"Like what? What do you need to know?"

"We want to get to know your father," she said.

"Tell us whatever you think we should know," Mr. Clark said.

At first, his thoughts scampered around like hard-shelled insects on a wooden floor.

"Take your time," Mrs. Clark said.

So, he did. He drank some of the coffee slowly, let sunlight from the room's big window hit his face, and then before he thought too much more, he started talking. What came out was a series of vignettes, wisdoms, and expressions all rendered in his father's voice. It was as if the him part of himself had shut down and the Pop part of himself had taken over. The him part of himself was sitting there along with the funeral director and the funeral director's wife listening to the story, too.

"You seem to have a knack for capturing a person. That's a special gift," Mr. Clark said, "a special gift, indeed."

"Pop would be proud," Mrs. Clark said, wiping a tear from the corner of one of her eyes. "And it is a special gift," she said, exchanging a glance with her husband.

When he was finished, he and Mr. Clark discussed the business end of the things, which Mr. Clark did politely and tactfully, respecting the little means which he and Pop had to spend on the viewing, the service, and the burial. Mr. Clark seemed able to bend numbers in a way that made everything he and Pop needed affordable. For that, he was grateful.

The viewing and funeral went smoothly. He sat proudly at the front of the room near the casket as people paraded by, paying their final respects. Pop was wearing the only suit he owned, and he looked alive—as much as he could—and happy. *I get prettier and prettier every day,* he heard his father say. A small number of Pop's friends from the tire factory where he worked showed up and brought cards filled with money for the Mortician. His aunt and uncle—the only living relatives he knew of on Pop's side—showed up and tried tending to him, but he hadn't seen them in years, and since he was 18, he did not want to accept their offer to live with them. But he took their card, which, he could tell just from holding it, was also filled with money. *Good for you, kid!* he heard his father say, laughing.

Soon the visitation was over, the guests gone. He sat alone in front of the funeral chapel, the sunlight that had been so insistent the past few days also gone. He loosened his black tie and patted the casket.

"Well, how did I do, Pop?" he asked. He waited for a response but heard nothing. "Pop?" he said. "Pop? Are you there?"

Still there was nothing. His self, which had been split, was now singular, the Pop part of himself having disappeared. He comforted himself by thinking about how Pop was already being reduced to molecules, and eventually, he would return to the elements that made those molecules. The elements, indestructible, would form new molecules, would nourish, would nurture. The whole world, after all, flourished on the backs of the dead.

A couple weeks later, when his father's affairs had mostly been settled, the phone rang. It was Mr. Clark. At first he was afraid Mr. Clark wanted more money. He would have some money from his father's life insurance eventually, and the money he had been given at the funeral was in the bank, so he had a cushion now, but none of that money would last forever. He just needed to finish his last couple months of school and find a decent job to get on his feet.

"Do you need a job?" Mr. Clark asked.

"I do, but I have to finish school, sir."

"That's OK—I know you have school. But we need a hand down here, part-time. Do you think you're the kind of man who can handle working in this type of environment? It isn't for everyone, but I think you can do it. I would understand, though, if you don't think it's for you."

"I can do it," the Mortician said, and even as he said it, he knew it was true.

He began shortly after that phone call, at first doing odd jobs around the funeral home—cleaning, running errands, setting up for services, but as more time passed, Mr. Clark taught him both the trade and the business of running the home. The more he learned, the more he liked it. It was a way to stay in the moment where the dead were always saying their last words, where no one was ever really lost. He felt he was doing exactly what he was supposed to be doing, and he considered himself lucky to have learned that so early in life.

One particular day in January when he was not working at Bells & Stone, he spent his free afternoon riding the Brown Line around Chicago. It was too cold to walk the streets, and riding the train made him feel like a film was speeding past him or like he was on a roller coaster. He secured a window seat, a packed lunch in his lap. At 4:30 p.m., he was listening to Louis Jordan and sinking his teeth into a ham sandwich when a woman sat down beside him. Discreetly, he pushed the stop button on his portable compact disc player but left his headphones on, as he often did so that he could try to submerge himself into the worlds of others, occasionally including himself in their conversations if appropriate. The woman next to him talked to the woman across the aisle from her.

They spoke in the staccato dialogue of those who have known each other a very long time. He had a hard time making out the particulars of their conversation above the din of the train, but what he did hear were names: *Gerald, Helen, Stella, Jesse*. Realizing there wasn't much else to glean from their conversation, he pushed play on his CD player and let horns and drums and guitars pull him down, down, down until he was molded into his seat. He came up for air only when the women exited the train a few stops later. He watched them walk away from the station, their arms locked, their steps in time. *They have to be related,* he thought.

He would not remember the names he had heard after the day was over, nor would he remember the faces of those two women, faces he would see again only in death, faces he would resurrect.

Chapter 9: Waiting for Boys

Making a baby was work. Stella had spent so much time protecting herself from pregnancy that she did not imagine trying to have a baby would be so difficult. But it was. Each month Stella embarked on a road of rough terrain, her emotions rising and falling with it. If her period was late, she was elated. But when a pregnancy test came back negative, she tumbled into a rocky well of heartbreak, the sides of which scratched her limbs all the way down.

Surely it hadn't taken Sarah this long to conceive. Sarah hadn't even been trying—it simply happened. As Stella struggled, she thought often and obsessively at times of Sarah, but she had never been able to bring herself to confront Gerald. It would only make things messier when really there was nothing to make a mess over. Sarah was sad and probably always would be. Gerald was a box in which she discarded this sadness. Still, Stella continued having Sarah cut her hair. She liked something about the woman's hands in her hair, the woman who had gotten—if only temporarily—what Stella wanted with Gerald. During their appointments, she spoke openly and frankly about the fact that she and Gerald wanted to have a baby, that they were trying, but she never called Gerald by name. Instead she littered her speech with the phrase *my husband* as liberally as a newlywed.

"My husband and I are hoping for a son," she had said two months earlier as Sarah sprayed hot water on her scalp. "We are already setting up the nursery," she fibbed.

"So you are pregnant now! Wow—congratulations. How far along are you?" Sarah asked.

Stella paused.

"Just a month," she lied.

It was a lie that would hold, she reasoned, until it became the truth or until she relented and started getting her hair done elsewhere.

One day in July, she sat on the back porch and smoked a cigarette, waiting for the results of another pregnancy test. As she breathed in and out, she contemplated the odds of actually being pregnant. It happened every day, and yet still the likelihood of it happening seemed so small. After nearly a year of trying, she and Gerald had talked on and off about adopting a child. But Gerald always said, "There's only so much that nurture can do." He was frightened of having a child whose genetics were unknown in the house with them. Stella held her cigarette up in front of her. Gerald would be angry if he knew she was smoking, less so, however, if he saw how her hand trembled in anticipation of what awaited her in the bathroom. She crushed the cigarette and walked into the house, light-headed.

"Quit it," she told her anxiety.

She closed her eyes and grabbed the pregnancy test, lifting it in front of her face, and then opening her eyes. Two blue lines populated the small window which before had been empty. Her hand shook as she double-checked the package to make sure what she thought was true actually was. Then she sank down on the floor, tears of relief running down her cheeks. She thought of Sarah, of the moment Sarah found out she was pregnant. Was this how Sarah had felt? Or had Sarah's tears been the hot tears of disgrace? *Disgrace*, she thought.

Stella's plan had always been to find a special way to tell Gerald she was pregnant, but now, gripped by emotion, she hurried to the phone in the kitchen and dialed the number to his office.

"I'm pregnant," she blurted out as soon as she heard his voice on the line.

There was a pause.

"Gerald?"

"I'm coming home," he said. He started talking to his secretary in the background.

"It's OK——we can..."

"Nope. I'm coming home to see my girl. I'll leave here in two hours at the most. I just have one more meeting."

"I love you so much."

"I love you, too."

When she hung up the phone, she went to her closet. She chose a yellow sundress——one of Gerald's favorites——to wear.

Then she put on makeup—the type of makeup she usually only wore at night: golden brown eyeshadow, black eyeliner, and red lipstick. She curled her hair, loose waves framing her face. She sprayed herself with perfume—her signature floral scent. When she finished getting ready, she still had time before Gerald's arrival. There was something else she needed to do. She called the salon and scheduled an appointment with Sarah for the next day. There was so much to talk about: the nursery, names, strollers. She would tell Sarah about it all, let her voice an opinion on diapers, cribs. She would inspect Sarah's face closely as the woman's hands worked through her hair. She would look for any sign of envy, and she would find it. Then she would never set foot in the salon again.

When Gerald arrived with a bouquet of daisies, Stella was lost in thought, one thigh crossed over the other, her foot moving in time with her imaginings. The sound of the door opening startled her, and she nearly ran into Gerald as he walked through the kitchen and into the living room where she had been sitting. He smelled lightly of sweat and clutched the flowers in his right hand.

"For me?" she said. She was nervous but didn't know why.

"For my little mama," he said, putting a heavy hand on her belly.

As they embraced, their hearts raced against one another, and Stella felt a tremble run through Gerald.

Before she could get a word out, "Are you scared?" he asked.

"I'm excited," she said. She pulled back and searched his face. "Are you scared?"

"No," he said. "Of course not." He paused, looking down. "Why would I be scared? I'm not scared at all."

She took him by the shoulders, pulling his body to hers. She rubbed the back of his head, his neck. He nestled into her, and for a second, she thought she felt him tremble again, as though he were suppressing tears. But then he stiffened and straightened up so that his chin rested atop her head.

"My little mama," he whispered.

During her pregnancy, Stella surrounded herself with women—namely Helen and her mother—because in their company she felt most at ease. After the sickness of the first trimester, her pregnancy went smoothly, and she adapted to her changing body happily. But when her due date came and went with no baby, she started to fear something could actually go wrong.

"Don't worry," her mother told her. "It's always that way with the first one. And with boys, too. Boys are always late."

She did worry though, and she could see worry in her mother's face and Helen's face, too. To cover their fear, they laughed, they fretted over final preparations for the baby's arrival. They cooked and froze food so Stella wouldn't have to prepare anything right after the baby came. They talked about what a good father Gerald would be.

"Better than your father ever was," her mother said.

"Wouldn't take much," Helen added.

Her mother sighed. No one even knew where their father was now that her mother had left. It was better that way, especially with the baby coming.

"No need to think about that now," her mother said. "About him." Then her mother grabbed her feet and started rubbing them. "Helen, take her shoulders," she said.

"See how much we spoil you," Helen said.

Stella squeezed Helen's hand as Helen kneaded her shoulders. Though she should have been trying to relax, she started thinking about boys, boys who grew into men, all the problems they could cause. It was hard to sit still. She shifted away from her mother and sister so that only she and the baby were touching.

"Let's listen to the radio," she said, standing abruptly and crossing the room to turn the music on.

A couple mornings later, just as their collective patience reached its limit, Stella's labor began. Helen had come over early and was helping Stella with some laundry. The first contraction arrived as she smoothed her hands over the flowers embroidered on the bottom of a hand towel. She shifted in her seat and thought maybe she needed to use the toilet, but then the pain intensified, moving in a wave from the top of her abdomen down. She winced and closed her eyes. When she opened them, Helen was holding a pair of Gerald's socks and staring at her.

"Stella?" she said. "Is it?"

"It's passed now."

"Should I call Gerald?"

"Not yet. There's time."

"Are you sure?"

"That's what mom said. She said there's always more time than you think."

"So, what do we do?"

"We wait. See if it keeps happening."

They fell silent for a few minutes, but Stella was starting to get scared. She glanced at her watch. Gerald had a meeting late that afternoon with one of his major clients. She wanted to call him, but she didn't want to do it before she was sure this was labor. When her friends had their first kids, there was always at least one false alarm.

"I'm going to get up and get some water," she said once she had finished folding her basket of laundry.

"I can get it for you."

"No, I'll get up."

In the kitchen, as she ran the tap, the pain returned, this time tightening around her body. She held her belly as water ran over the edge of the glass and down her hand.

"Are you OK?" Helen asked.

"Just put something on the TV," Stella said.

"Don't you think——"

"There's still time," she said.

Helen helped Stella back into the living room where they spent the next hour pretending to watch re-runs of *I Love Lucy*. Helen tried to talk Stella through the pain, but it increased in intensity and frequency.

"I'm calling Gerald now," Helen said firmly.

Stella could only nod, gripping the arm of the couch until she thought she would tear the fabric with her fingernails.

Helen picked up the phone from the end table and dialed Gerald's office. "Hello, is Gerald available?...Oh, he is? I see. Well, his wife needs him immediately. Where can he be reached?"

"Helen——it's OK. We'll go and he can meet us there," Stella said.

Helen widened her eyes at Stella and put her hand over the bottom of the phone.

"I am going to find him," she hissed and then turned her attention back to the call. "Listen. His wife is in labor. That means Gerald is needed at home. We need to know how to find him and now."

As much as Stella would have never condoned rudeness to Gerald's secretary who had become a friend of hers, she was secretly delighted by Helen's clipped tone and continued interrogation. In the space between contractions, she started to laugh.

Helen hung up the phone. "What's so funny?"

"You."

"What?"

"You're the best damn sister in the world, you know that?"

"I know." Helen laughed, beaming. "But more importantly, Gerald's on his way to a meeting. The woman said she'd call where he's going and let him know what is happening."

"So he'll meet us at the hospital, right?"

Helen nodded.

"And Mom?"

"We'll call her from the hospital, too."

"There's no rush, Helen, really. I'm sure there's no rush. We can..." Another contraction seized her, and she gripped her sister's hand. "Let's go," she said.

In the car, Helen turned on the classical music station, and Stella didn't know if Helen had done that for Stella's benefit or her own. But it seemed to keep them both calm and focused, and as it played, Stella leaned her head against the window, watching as the music elevated bored streets into beauty.

"Helen?"

"Yes, are you OK?"

"This is the last time it's going to be just me like this."

"I know."

"Everything's changing again."

"We talked about that. It's OK."

"You're right. It's all going to be OK," she said as they pulled in the hospital parking lot. "It has to all be OK."

But once she was settled in a room on the labor and delivery floor, Stella worried about Gerald. Every so often she asked Helen to walk out to the hallway and then back down to the lobby just in case. After the third time, Helen said no.

"He'll be here. Don't worry."

"It just doesn't feel right."

"He might be in traffic. Or he may not have gotten the message yet."

"I'm sure he got the message."

"All that should be the least of your worries right now. You know him. If he's anything he's reliable, right?"

"You're right." She patted the space beside her in the hospital bed. "Sit with me, will you?" she said.

Helen sat down as Stella held out her hand. Helen took it, squeezing it once, twice. And then they waited quietly for the boys to come.

Chapter 10: Departures, Arrivals

Traffic had been horrible coming back from the city. Gerald had not gotten the message that Stella was in labor until he stopped back at the office after eating dinner with his clients. Immediately he turned around and headed to the hospital in Naperville, cursing himself for not sending someone else to the meeting in his place, though he couldn't have known. On the way there, an accident obstructed two lanes of traffic on I-88, and he was forced to crawl toward his wife and child.

When he finally arrived at Edward Hospital, his stomach dropped. Fire trucks surrounded the building. Sirens screamed on Osler Drive, blocking the entrance into the parking lot. He got as close as he could, and then, crazed and desperate, parked haphazardly on the street. Unaware of anything but the need to find his wife, he ran toward the building, nearly getting hit by a car as he crossed the street.

At first he had only worried about missing the birth of his son. Now he worried that he was no longer going to be a father at all. Doctors, nurses, patients, police officers, and firefighters were gathered in groups around the building. A plume of gray smoke billowed from the first floor. For a second Gerald was overwhelmed, nearly paralyzed, but he shook it off and approached the first police officer he could find.

"My wife," he said. "I need to find my wife."

"OK, son," the cop said. He looked near retirement age and chewed gum. "OK." He chomped on his gum.

Gerald stared at him blankly, waiting.

"Now, why was she, your wife, why was she here?"

"She's having a baby."

"A baby. Oh, congratulations. Boy or a girl?"

"Boy——I just need to find them. What's going on?"

"Everything's OK, son. We'll find her."

"But what happened?"

"You smell smoke?"

"I get it——there was a fire."

"You're going to be a fine father after all, son," he patted Gerald on the shoulder and laughed.

This didn't seem like a time to crack a stupid joke. Gerald forced his voice into politeness. "OK——what should I do? What's the protocol?"

"Ask someone wearing scrubs. They'll help you out."

Gerald nodded and beelined for the first person in scrubs he saw.

"Good luck being a dad, son. You're going to need it!" the officer called out.

The man in scrubs stood with his arms crossed, staring at the building.

"Excuse me," Gerald said. "Can you help me find my wife? She's here having a baby. Stella Drozka is her name. She's having a boy."

"Come with me," he said, leading Gerald around the side of the building. "There was a grease fire in the kitchen, but it looks worse than it is. All the patients are safe and sound. See the doctor over there?" He pointed toward another man in scrubs. "That's Dr. Reese. He works on labor and delivery. You walk right over to him and ask him where the labor and delivery patients are."

"Thank you. Thank you so much," Gerald said, blinking back against tears of relief as he walked toward the man he had been directed to.

"Can you help me? I'm trying to find my wife. She is here having a baby. Stella Drozka is her name. She's having a boy."

"Baby boy? Named Jesse?"

"Yes, yes that's what we were going to name him."

The doctor smiled widely. "Let's go."

Gerald followed the doctor through the crowd, his mouth dry and his heart racing. The doctor led him to a back door of the hospital and then up two flights of stairs. They walked down a hallway where pictures of mothers and babies and infant-themed décor hung on the walls. Finally, they stopped at a room, and Gerald followed the doctor in. A curtain blocked his view of the bed.

"Someone is here to see you," the doctor said, pulling the curtain back a little.

He gestured for Gerald to move forward. Behind the curtain were Helen and Stella and the baby. Stella lay in bed with the baby swaddled in her arms, and Helen stood next to her, a hand on her shoulder.

"I'm here, Stella. I'm so sorry. Traffic——"

Stella looked up at him and smiled so beautifully that he stopped talking. "It's OK, honey. We're all OK," she said. She held the baby up to him. "This is Jesse, honey. He's got 10 fingers and 10 toes and 2 healthy lungs. And Helen was here with me the whole time." She smiled at Helen, who looked flatly at Gerald.

"I'm sorry——I shouldn't have gone to the meeting. Or to dinner after. I should have stayed close."

"Everything is all right. Take your son. Hold our boy."

And then, as the hospital struggled to return to normality, Gerald took his son into his arms. He stared into his son's face and touched the boy's tiny nose. The boy started to cry, and Gerald held him so that the baby's head leaned against his shoulder. "Shhh," he said, "There, there, little one." He buried his face in the boy's blanket, and for a second, he smelled smoke. Sarah's face flashed in his mind, though he tried not to think of her, though he wished she would stop writing. He couldn't help but think of her now, and of his other son, Jesse's brother, who never was. Tears rocked his body, sending waves through the delicate architecture of his son.

"Are you OK?" Stella asked. She reached out from where she lay and touched his hip.

"I'm so happy," he said. "I'm just so happy."

Chapter 11: On the Ward

During Stella's pregnancy, Helen watched her sister's body grow and change so intimately that it was almost as if the pregnancy belonged to them both. But after Stella gave birth to Jesse, that feeling withered. It was Stella's breasts at which the baby nursed and between her tending and Gerald's hovering, Helen was displaced, a refugee.

She spent most of her time alone, and the more time she spent alone, the less desire she had to see anyone. When that summer slipped into fall and the air assumed its cool, Helen's level of agitation increased. Anger festered inside her, and she lashed out where she could——store clerks, fellow El passengers, coworkers, all of them endured cold looks and biting comments. She wished to drive people away from her——to watch them flee as she cut through their tide. She didn't know where the anger came from, but she knew it started as a dream she had swallowed, a dream that had been eaten away. Where once there had been fruit, now there was only a stone.

Aside from the fact that she was no one's wife and no one's mother, she had no career. Her job as a file clerk at the hospital only fomented her anger. All day she retrieved files and then put them away again. Her fingertips were permanently dry, and in the winter, they cracked. She saw virtually no rewards for her labor. Occasionally someone gave her a special thanks because she had done this or that in a timely fashion. But really, her work was something that could not even make a shadow in a sunlit room. It was dangerous doing work you couldn't see. It meant you had either lost sight of something bigger or had never seen anything in the first place.

She had always wanted to be something, somebody. She had looked through junior college course catalogs. She had listened to suggestions from Stella, Gerald, and her mother about what to do. But every time she got set on something, she froze. She had gotten as far as registering for an accounting program, but when she thought about school, about all the people she'd have to talk to, the work she'd have to do, she just got so tired. The first day of classes came and went, and she continued on at the hospital.

One day, all of it simply imploded, the stone detonating inside her. It was a quiet disaster, like watching a nuclear bomb blast on a television with the sound off. She sat down in an aisle of files——the "S" aisle——and stared at the paper in front of her. She had been looking for a woman named Anna Schmidt's file. She couldn't find it, no matter how many times she pulled all the Schmidts out, all the SCHs. Soon pictures of Anna Schmidt began to float in front of her, a woman she imagined to be tall with long blonde hair and full, red lips. A woman her junior who had a whole life full of dreams that had not yet gone to stone, a woman whose father hadn't screamed at her mother, a woman whose grandfather had never touched her, a woman who would have real babies, not dolls. It wasn't just Anna Schmidt, however. The shelves were filled with the files of other women, faceless name after faceless name. She imagined all of them glowing—happy and healthy people who did what they wanted without fear or regret.

She did not know how long she had been sitting on the floor, but suddenly a pair of feet was approaching her; the feet were connected to legs, and the legs disappeared beneath a sensible wool skirt.

"Helen?" a voice from above asked. "Helen, are you OK?"

Helen looked up, but the face above her was obscured by a halo of light. She squinted, putting a hand on her brow against it.

"Helen, let me help you up," the voice said.

She looked at the floor; the files were spilled around her feet.

"Helen. Helen, are you OK? Did you fall?" the voice said.

Helen looked up again, and she thought she shook her head, but the voice did not say anything else, so she was unsure whether or not she had actually moved.

"Carol," the voice said, "call up to the ER. Something's wrong with Helen."

After a few minutes, Helen felt herself being lifted by a pair of strong arms. She slapped the arms at first, but it became apparent she was no match for them as they carried her up and into a wheelchair. Soon she was in the corridors of the hospital, the well-known pathways now exotic as the wind of her motion caused her hair to billow.

For a second, it felt pleasant.

In the ER, nurses dressed her in a gown and put a bracelet with her name and birthdate on her wrist. They measured her blood pressure and drew her blood. They tried talking to her, but each time she snapped at them. "I'm fine. I'm just fucking fine," she heard herself repeating. She did not feel dazed as she had back in the file room; now she felt nothing.

Eventually, a doctor came in, a tall, dark-haired man with a face just off kilter enough to be trusted. He smiled and held out his hand, and she stared at it, then looked away.

"Not a hand shaker, are you?" he said. "Well, I'm Dr. Smythe."

"Yeah? Good for you."

"How are you feeling, Helen?"

She said nothing.

He drew in a sharp breath.

"I'll give it to you one more time: how are you feeling?" he said, drawing out the words.

"Fine. I'm goddamn fine."

He sat on a stool with wheels on the bottom and wheeled himself to the side of her bed. He smelled strongly of cologne and faintly of tobacco.

"Can you tell me what happened to you before you came here?"

"I was working."

"That's what I heard. But can you tell me more about what exactly happened to you? You weren't talking then. Did you fall down? Do you think you lost consciousness?"

"They already asked me that. I said no."

"So, you didn't lose consciousness?"

"No."

He got up and pulled the door shut. "Helen," he said turning around, "I need you to be absolutely honest with me." He paused. "Have you been depressed—or maybe, maybe something happened recently that put you under an abnormal amount of stress?"

Helen stared at the ceiling as tears filled the basins around her eyes. It was impossible to explain. The dreams and stones, the files and failures. And then there was gravity, the constant force pulling her deeper toward the center of the earth, a force so jealous that it refused to let her go even a little. All she could do was sink, letting her lungs fill with soil and heat.

"Helen?" Dr. Smythe said. He waited. "All right." He looked at the nurse. "We need to transfer her."

"Linden Oaks?"

"Linden Oaks."

They moved Helen to a small, private room in Linden Oaks, a part of the hospital given that name to disguise its function as a mental health facility. Shortly after Helen was transferred, Stella came, but Helen refused the visit. For the first time, even the thought of her sister gave her no comfort. She imagined Stella at the nurse's station. *What? She would never do that. You have to let me see her,* Stella would say. *I'm sorry, ma'am. She said absolutely no visitors, family included.* Helen should have felt guilty, but she didn't. The inside of her was white, pure nothing. Mostly, she slept. When she wasn't sleeping, she counted things in the room——ceiling tiles, marks on the walls, the number of people she heard walk by——until she fell asleep again.

On her second morning there, Dr. Smythe reappeared. "Hi Helen," he said.

She sat in a chair looking out the window. She had spent the last hour staring off into the trees outside her window. Every so often a bird landed and then flew away. When it flew away, she felt worse than she had before it left.

"I hear you still haven't done much talking," the doctor said.

"Nothing to say," Helen said, still staring out the window.

"I highly doubt that," he said. "Say, Helen, I was wondering if I could buy you lunch."

"But the food here is phenomenal."

"Was that a joke?"

"Does a cat have an ass?" she said.

A small sparrow landed on the branch nearest her.

"If I had known you were funny, I would have come yesterday."

"Sorry to disappoint."

"That was a joke, too."

"You had to come eventually anyway," Helen said, turning away from the window and toward him.

"No, I didn't. I came because I wanted to see if you were OK."

"I'm fine."

"You aren't going to be fine if you don't start being more communicative. If you don't even let your sister in, who will help you? Who will you talk to?"

"I told you already there's nothing to say."

"I don't believe you."

"I don't want to eat lunch with you."

"Fine. Do you care if I eat?"

"No."

He pulled an orange out of his pocket and began peeling it. The scent of citrus exploded in the air.

"Everyone has a story," he said and licked his finger. "And I believe everyone's story is both valid and valuable."

"Yeah? What's yours, doctor? Did you grow up in a house with columns out front, go to a fancy college with lots of friends, and now it's all life-saving heroics, adorable kids, beautiful wife?"

"There are a lot of assumptions packed into that statement. You know what one of my high school teachers used to say?" He paused and put a slice of orange into his mouth. "You're an ass if you assume things. Or at the very least, you sound like one."

He threw his orange peels in the garbage. Then he pulled up a chair next to hers and sat so that they both faced the window.

"Full disclosure, I never liked that teacher very much," he said.

Helen watched as he picked a bit of orange skin from his teeth. It was endearing somehow, even though she knew he was trying to break her open.

"One of those real crotchety old guys, you know? Everything I didn't want to be when I became a doctor."

She counted the birds that landed and then flew away, listening to the slight rattle in his breath as they sat there.

"I suppose I should go. I like sitting here, but I'll be in trouble if they know I'm just watching the birds with you."

He stood and moved his chair away from her. As she heard the chair slide across the floor tiles, 1-2-3-4, she panicked. Her internal expanse of white had begun to color at the edges. She turned toward him, her heart beating in sixteenth notes. She had carried so much for so long, and she had been alone forever, it seemed.

"I'll talk to you," she blurted out, "If you stay, I'll talk."

He sat back down, and Helen cleared her throat. Slowly, like a ribbon, Helen's story, all of it, unspooled into his ears.

Chapter 12: Born of Fire

Jesse liked guns. He liked their weight, their tangibility, and their precision. As a teenager, he hung posters not of bands or girls but posters of guns in his room—framed prints detailing various models of Colts, Smith & Wessons, Brownings, each in full color and proudly labeled. Guns were good company. They only spoke when spoken to. They did not ask anything of anyone. They were silent, steel dogs who did not eat or shit but heeled their masters, waiting on hips, on shoulders to be called to action. In return, they were loved, revered. Jesse felt better surrounded by them. As he fell asleep looking at the guns, he promised himself that one day he would own every last one of them.

He remembered the first time he witnessed a gun do the will of its master. It was on a trip into the city with his mother. They had missed their stop on the El and ended up in a part of Chicago his mother said made her "uncomfortable," though Jesse did not know where they were. She made him hold her hand as they walked despite it making him feel silly since he was 10 and too old to do so. His mother held her head high as they walked down the dimly lit street, passing through thin groves of men who talked loudly, some with bottles in paper bags, some who sat on the sidewalks, occasionally wiping their noses on the backs of their hands or asking for money. She ignored the conversations and pulled him along toward where they would get on another train to take them back downtown where Jesse's father waited. But Jesse had to go to the bathroom and so his mother stopped at a small bar——the only open thing on the street and brought him inside.

The place was dark and filled with men smoking cigarettes back-to-back. A large red neon sign reading "ACE" in block letters hung on the back wall. Under its light, he walked into the bathroom and did his business, his feet stepping carefully around a few small, shallow pools of urine left by drunken patrons, poor aim their tell.

When he finished, he walked out and looked for his mother but did not see her anywhere. He was not frightened by her absence; rather, he was emboldened by it. He was suddenly responsible for himself, a vague concept he had desired for some time. So, he walked outside and into the thrill and disgust of a city night. He turned down an alley, dark and tumorous, conscious that at any moment his freedom could be taken by his mother's strong hands.

At the far end of the alley, he saw two men standing, one in a derby cap and the other in a red ski jacket, their bodies tense. He could not understand what they were saying, but he could sense anger in the tenor of their speech. The man in the red jacket pushed the man in the derby cap, who stumbled back a little, and then pulled a silver pistol from inside his coat, which caught the alley light.

It was the first gun Jesse remembered loving.

The man in the red ski jacket backed against the wall the moment the gun came uncloaked. The man in the derby cap steadily pointed the gun at the other man's head for a moment until in one fluid motion, he brought the butt of it down on the other man's nose with a beautifully dull thud. Blood sprayed from his face, the droplets fine and black. The man in the derby cap spun away; Jesse watched the hem of his coat swing as he retreated. The farther the man and that gun were from Jesse, the less safe he felt. The man who held it had seemed untouchable.

As the man in the red ski jacket lay in the alley, Jesse turned and headed around the corner where he saw his mother frantically talking to a man outside the bar. Jesse approached her only half-present, seeing the gun, the blood, over and over again.

"Mom," he said, ice in his voice, "I'm right here."

"Damn it, Jesse," she said. "Where did you go?"

He knew he should lie now, but he was not living in this moment; he was alive in the moment of the man's nose spraying blood, in the first moment of violence he had witnessed.

"I went on a walk," he said.

"You don't wander off, Jesse. You don't walk away from me here. Do you understand?" she said.

He did not lift his eyes to hers.

"Do you understand?" she asked again, her hands rough on his chin.

"Yes."

"Say it again."

"I said yes."

She continued holding his chin until it hurt, and while he should have felt guilty, he did not feel guilty. He was satisfied at having exercised a burgeoning independence. Something important had just happened to him, something he wanted to think of on his own terms. He did not want anyone to tell him the men were bad. He wanted to think independently about the men, the gun. He wanted to replay the incident over and over in his mind. In the days, months, and years to come, he would—sometimes casting himself as the man in the driver's cap, and sometimes as the gun itself, steeled and righteous, an instrument of will.

It would be years, of course, before he ever handled a gun. His father did not have much interest in guns and never owned one. But as Jesse grew up and expressed interest in them, his father endeavored to as well, although he did not own any. Every year Jesse looked forward to his birthday, thinking that year might be the one which would bring him a wrapped box containing a rifle, a pistol, but every year he received some other indulgent item—video game consoles, high-quality headphones, sports equipment—in which he took no pleasure. He thinly veiled his disappointment just as his father thinly veiled his own at seeing that Jesse did not like the gift. But finally on Jesse's 16th birthday, his father engineered a compromise so neither of them was disappointed. He arranged for Jesse to take a gun safety class and brought him to a shooting range.

The man working at the range, Bud, took one look at Jesse, removed the cigar from between his lips and said, "This is a pistol man, right here." Jesse's eyes lit up, for all he wanted was to shoot a gun like the one he had seen in that alley when he was a boy.

Bud set both Jesse and his father up with pistols, Smith & Wesson .45s. Targets hung before them—black human forms with white x's on the chests. White lines radiated out from the x's with numbers on them.

"You always aim low," Bud said, holding his own pistol and lining up the sights. "Just put the bead in the sight and then aim a little low. Breathe out and squeeze the trigger. You take a couple shots, you get the feel for your pistol, and then you two'll be a pair."

He stood close behind Jesse as Jesse lined up the sights for his first shot. Jesse's hands trembled slightly. He wanted to do well; he wanted his bullet to hit its mark.

"Easy does it, kid. Take a deep breath and exhale," Bud said. "That's it."

Jesse squeezed the trigger. While he did not hit the x, his bullet struck near it.

"Good shooting, kid!" Bud slapped his shoulder.

"Nice work," his dad said, staring at the target.

Though he remembered feeling proud of his first shot, it was not his first shot that Jesse thought about most. The shot he took when Bud and his father were distracted by talking was what he dwelled upon. He was finally alone with a gun, which he called to heel, carefully lining up the sights on the heart of the target and exhaling to keep his hands steady at the bottom of his breath. Then he squeezed the trigger, his hand recoiling slightly as the bullet pierced the heart of its victim, a perfect hole right where he had aimed. It was as though he had somehow traveled through the gun, as though part of him had struck the mark. He felt strong, stronger than he had ever felt before.

"Damn fine shot, kid!" Bud said when he and Jesse's father finished talking.

Jesse smiled. His father, whose mouth was slightly ajar, nodded absently while staring at the holes in Jesse's target.

Although his father would never buy him a gun and he did not enjoy the range, his father still took him once a month where they shot off rounds until Jesse gave the signal that he had his fill. After each trip, Jesse's hunger was more honed, and he and his father went to restaurants where he tore through steaks, burgers, anything red, bloody.

Now grown with guns unfettered around his apartment, his hunger still peaked after shooting, but instead of going out, he cooked food the way he liked it: choice cuts of beef, seared and then broiled, tender enough to cut with a butter knife.

Chapter 13: Everything That Ever Was

Helen believed everything that ever was still is, even if it was slightly out of her periphery. Thinking this way made life easier. It meant no decision was ever final. It meant she had never done anything wrong because every moment before every decision still existed somewhere—she would only have to be tuned to the right frequency to find it.

Being in possession of this philosophy, she did not regret quitting her job at the hospital after she was released from Linden Oaks, nor did she regret moving into a smaller, more affordable one bedroom. Instead of finding a new full-time job, she had been working for a temp agency, which gave her the freedom to work if and when she pleased. Overall, this lack of consistency was a better match for her. She had more time alone to think, to read, to dream of all the things she would never do. And her new building, though it had its flaws, was tidy and warm, its smell familiar, reminiscent of the scent of her dolls.

As the days passed quietly, Helen cultivated a small existence and then smaller still. She eliminated nearly all her possessions—paring down her belongings until only essential items remained. She had two place settings of dishes and two drinking glasses of each type: juice, whiskey, wine, water. She had a few pots and pans, pieces of furniture, towels, and wash cloths. For clothes, she wore only dresses, even in the winter. The dresses were carefully curated by season and purpose, each unique in form and function. This one for a cloudy day and this one for a sunny afternoon; this one for work and this one for pleasure. When at rest, the dresses hung in her closet, arranged carefully by color, making her closet the brightest place in the apartment.

Another thing she eliminated from her life was people. She never had many to begin with, but after getting out of the hospital and moving into this little cove, she did not reach out to them and frequently ignored even Stella's calls. At one time she had yearned for certain connections, but now those things seemed out of reach. She had been marked, she thought, from a young age. Her grandfather's transgressions perspired onto her, and she stunk of them still. Since they had been his actions and not hers, she could not change the moment before them. Only the moments of the transgressions existed, and she had existed in those moments for so long that she did not know how to stop. It was lonely living in the past and present simultaneously; she was split between two places at once and could not give full attention to either. But being alone was a comfort: she never had to explain anything to anyone.

One day a knock sounded on her door, and she first mistook it for a knock on her neighbor's door. But when she heard it a second time and then a third, she knew it was her door being knocked upon. Unnerved, she looked through the peephole, her palm around the doorknob.

Outside stood a man who appeared to be in his late 30s, her age, or perhaps slightly younger. His hair was thick, black, greased. He looked like he had walked out of her high school years, which made him seem familiar, somehow safe.

Helen opened the door just enough to put her face in the doorway.

"Can I help you?" she said.

"Steven," he said, putting his hand forward.

Helen looked down at his hand and then up at his face.

"I live down the hall." His hand was still extended.

"Oh, OK. I'm Helen," she said, opening the door wider and taking his hand.

"Nice to meet you. So, Helen, I did something dumb. I just moved in yesterday, and I managed to lock myself out already. I was wondering if I could use your phone to call the landlord."

"All right," she said, keeping her body firmly planted between him and the rest of the apartment.

"Can I come in?" He smiled.

"Yes, sure——sorry." She pulled the door open fully, slowly moving to the side.

He walked past her and immediately began to survey the apartment, further unnerving Helen who stood near the open door.

"It's nice in here," he said. "Uncluttered, clean."

"Is it just like yours?"

"Pretty much, except mine doesn't look like an organized woman lives in it."

"I see."

"I mean that as a compliment."

"Noted."

"Seriously," he said. "It's cozy in a spartan way."

Helen cleared her throat. "The phone is over there," she said, pointing to a round end table on which a white cordless phone was the only thing.

He walked toward the phone and then stopped and turned back toward her.

"Sorry—do you have the landlord's number? I know, I know. What else am I going to ask you for, right?"

Helen looked back at the door, which was still open, and then forward at Steven. He was smiling at her, his eyes warm gems. She closed the door and retrieved an address book from a drawer in the kitchen.

"Here," she said, spreading the pages apart. "Right here."

She pulled her fingers from the book as soon as she could to avoid touching his. After he dialed, she walked toward the front door, looking for something to fumble with so she didn't appear to be listening to his conversation.

When he hung up the phone, she turned around.

"He's coming by soon."

"Good."

"Mind if I stick around for a few minutes?"

Helen did mind. She did not want a foreign presence in her apartment, but it would be unneighborly, rude to send him back out to wander the hallway while he waited for their notoriously tardy landlord.

"The landlord is always late," she said. "You should know that about him."

"Thanks. I appreciate the tip. So, does that mean I can stay?"

Helen looked at her feet and exhaled.

"Sure. Have a seat."

She pointed toward the one chair in the room. She didn't want him to sit on the sofa, for it was closest to the door, and she wanted to be closest to the door. It was not that she thought he was dangerous, or perhaps it was that she thought he was—but the danger was not physical or immediate. It was the same danger any human interaction presented. Anyone was capable of doing anything at any time.

They made small talk for a while; mainly Steven talked, and Helen listened and smiled. He talked about his work fixing roads, he talked about how he came to live in the building, he talked about the neighborhood bars he liked. Men like Steven always seemed to appreciate a woman's silence, and silence was much of what Helen had to give. Silence allowed a man to be whoever he wanted—larger than himself, an authority, a star. Though she could tell he was a talker, he had a quality she had wished for her whole life: confidence.

"What about you? Tell me about you," he said finally.

But thankfully the landlord knocked on the door, and Helen was spared from having to talk about herself. She shut the door behind Steven, both relieved and sad. Her apartment, which she loved for its smallness, felt too big, its emptiness glaring. Being alone, she reminded herself, meant she would always know what to expect. Having grown up the way she did, surrounded by men like fireworks, she liked knowing what would happen next.

A few days later, Helen returned from work to find a note beneath her door. It was from Steven. He wanted her to come over to his apartment for coffee that evening. She walked through the catalogue of her mind looking for an excuse to turn down his invitation. She hadn't gone on a date in years—not since Gerald and Stella dragged her on a double date with one of Gerald's friends, a man with soft hands, a man who touched her too often on the first date. She didn't like the way he smelled.

"He's a good guy. Give him another chance. He was really nervous. You know I care about you. I wouldn't introduce you to someone I thought wasn't good enough for you. We're family after all," Gerald had said.

"I don't want to see him again."

"Seriously? I already invited him for cocktails."

"I said no."

"Gerald, it's OK. I'll talk to him if you want," Stella said.

Helen could feel them exchanging looks, but she didn't care.

"I'm sorry. I don't mean to be that way," Gerald said as she walked away. She threw a hand up behind her, and neither Stella nor Gerald had tried to set her up with anyone since.

This was different though—this was organic. Although she hated to admit it, she was curious. She was curious about what his apartment looked like and what would happen if she spent more time with him. She let herself fathom having her own person, a thought she did not often allow herself to indulge in. *Could I like him?* she asked herself. She was attracted to him, she supposed—as much as she had ever been attracted to any man—so she answered *yes* to her own question, walked down the hall on weak legs, and knocked on his door.

His apartment was what she had expected: mismatched, shabby. But there was something comfortable about it. She liked the way it smelled—bar soap and musk. They sat at his small kitchen table, and Steven began talking. He was full of stories. He had traveled extensively and was just now settling back in Illinois. She liked to listen to him; she liked to follow along. It made her feel like part of something.

"You don't talk much, do you?" he said.

"I talk when I have something to say."

"I like that about you. There aren't enough people like that."

"No, there aren't," she managed.

And then they were silent for a moment, a moment in which Helen felt something like confidence, even if it was temporary.

Over the few weeks, she and Steven visited each other and spent hours drinking weak coffee, talking, or watching TV. While she supposed she should have been happy about spending time with someone, being around him mainly made her anxious. She did not ask him for anything; she waited for him to come to her, which he did, repeatedly, but she could not shake the feeling that one day he would simply disappear. He would go somewhere else, to someone else. And her apartment would resume the feeling it had when he left that first day, a largeness she wasn't big enough to fill.

Helen by no means prided herself a cook, but she could make a few things well. Steven was coming to dinner, and she decided to make pasta with red sauce and garlic bread and a salad, of course, for she didn't believe in eating a meal without vegetables of some kind. She was barefoot and wore a sleeveless blue cotton A-line dress, one of her favorites for its simplicity. She was putting dinner on the table when he knocked on the door.

She opened it, and he held out a bottle of red wine.

"Pretty dress on a pretty lady," he said.

She shook her head and turned away. "I'm going to open the wine."

"I mean it. It's pretty."

"Thanks," she said, pouring them each a glass of wine. "I don't wear pants unless I have to."

"Interesting philosophy."

"Anybody can wear pants," she said.

"I'm living proof. But I have a specific pants system. I buy one pair of Levi's and wear them until they're done. Then I buy another pair. One new pair in, one old pair out. For every single thing I bring into my apartment, I try to throw something else out."

"Many women might not be impressed by that, but I like it." She laughed as she gestured to a seat, and they both sat down and started serving themselves. She drank half a glass of wine quickly. The alcohol relaxed her, and she relinquished her carefully cultivated restraint. "People have too many things. Little stupid things made out of plastic. Three kinds of this. Two kinds of that," she said. "And I just imagine it in the trash. I imagine all of it in a landfill, sitting there for years and years and years. It bothers me. All that waste because someone needed a trinket or a bottle of this or that." Then she caught herself and started eating to avoid talking too much.

"I knew you had some hellfire in you." Steven winked. "I agree with you. I grew up in the country——not on a farm, really, but it was an old house on some acreage in Wisconsin. The people who lived there before us used to dump garbage on the property. All summer we'd find things they had buried——ink bottles, milk bottles, a doll's head. It was like living on a graveyard."

"Or an archaeological site," she said.

"That's a better way of looking at it." He put down his fork. "You know what? This is one of the best dinners I ever ate," he said.

"Bullshit," Helen said.

"I mean it," he said.

He looked so serious that Helen had no choice but to believe him.

"Well, thank you."

"No, thank you," he said, drawing the *you* out. He held her gaze, his lower lip shiny from the butter on the garlic bread, and smiled.

After the meal was over and the dishes had been cleared, they sat on the couch with the wine, finishing the bottle.

"So if you don't wear pants, how many dresses do you have?" he asked, his cheeks red with cabernet.

"A lot."

"How many?"

"I don't know. I don't ever throw them out."

"So where are they?"

"You want to know where my dresses are?"

"Yes, where are your dresses? Show me your dresses." He tapped her kneecap with his index finger.

"Why?"

"I'm curious."

"Strange thing to be curious about."

"I want to know what I'm getting into."

Helen looked straight into his eyes, her mouth slightly pinched. She swallowed the rest of her wine and then stood up and walked into the bedroom without saying anything. She heard him follow as she knew he would. A pang of anxiety shot through her. Was this just a line to get into her bedroom? She wanted to turn around, to push him out, but when she looked back over her shoulder, he smiled so sincerely, so much like a boy, she couldn't do it.

Her closet faced the bed and was long with two sliding doors. She turned on the light and pulled both the doors open so that all the dresses were illuminated, a spectrum of reds, blues, blacks, greens, whites, yellows, and in-betweens that swept across the length of the space. Flowers grew up from hems. Stripes wound their way around bodices. Polka dots scattered themselves across smart a-lines. There were long dresses and short dresses and nighttime dresses and daytime dresses, dresses made from cotton, lace, satin.

It was like giving something up, showing this to him, and having laid herself bare, she sat on the bed and watched him. He stared at all the dresses and then as though he could not help himself, he walked down the length of the closet, his fingertips grazing fabric after fabric in the same delicate way he had touched her knee. When he finished one pass, he turned and made another, lingering in each well of the color palate.

When he was done, he sat next to her, staring at the open closet.

"I think I'm in love with you," he said.

For a moment neither of them spoke. They merely watched the silent dresses, until Steven took her hand in his and opened her palm to his cheek.

She closed her eyes. She let his cheek rest in her hand. His quiet let her know he was sincere. But then the panic returned, and her mind started moving. She could see the future: they would spend nights in bed, their possessions merged——his t-shirts and socks forming cotton settlements in her territory, his one pair of Levi's draped across the chair in the bedroom each night. She thought about all the things she would have to tell him if she were to move toward this future. There was too much, the decisions made for her so long ago that could not be undone, the moments she could not stop living in. It was impossible to live in all three tenses, and she was already committed to two: the past and the present, which galloped in opposite directions nearly pulling her apart.

She took her hand away.

"I think you should go."

Steven looked at her, a pilgrim astonished by his own failure to reach the land in which he wished to worship.

"Really, you better go." She walked toward the front door. "I'm sorry," she said as she held the door open for him.

"I don't understand——what did I do?" he asked.

"Nothing. It's nothing. Please just go," she said.

He shook his head and walked out. She watched him disappear down the hall. The feel of his face on her palm rang across its lines. *It will only hurt for a little while*, she told herself as she shut the door. *And then it will be better.*

Chapter 14: Heroes

Not unlike his parents who often spent their evenings reading——his father, science magazines and journals; his mother, novels and stories——Jesse digested stories. At first, he read novels of war, but when he entered his mid to late teens, he sought out studies of different types of violence, bloody demarcations between the self and others, *A Feast of Snakes*, *The Killer Inside Me*. As he read, he thought, and as he thought, he wrote in his journal. He did not consider himself a writer, but he wrote because he thought things no one would understand. These thoughts separated him from his friends and his parents. But when he wrote them down, the gap lessened and he was able to sit comfortably in a room with other people and smile and laugh and genuinely feel he belonged to the human race, not to some alien race of which he was the only living remnant.

He guarded the journals with his life.

I believe in the gun, he wrote, *in the power and the holiness of the gun. I believe in violence. I believe in the necessity of violence to restore the world to a state of equilibrium.* To him, it was not disease or famine or natural disaster that would save the world from its own arrogance: it was violence.

Violence in some form had always and would always shape the landscape of the world. People were conquered. Civilizations rose up and then crumbled. Nations were built and destroyed. The lines of the modern world owed their existence to violence. *There are those in society who are killers. The killers who were blessed with a sense of right and wrong, those who had good homes and good parents, we are the lucky ones. We become soldiers because there is no place we can become ourselves other than in the freedom and discipline of the service. The rest of the killers, well, those are the people you see on the covers of newspapers and magazines. Those are ones everyone else is afraid of. Their violence is a different brand altogether. Their motivations aren't pure.* It wasn't that he woke in the morning with the urge to kill. It was that he knew something inside himself would flounder and die if he never put himself in the way of the gun, the way of righteousness, an agent of equilibrium.

When the Twin Towers fell on September 11, 2001, Jesse was 25 years old. The Towers falling, he thought, was a great endeavor at equalizing. Death to avenge the already dead. Financial blows to the wealthiest of the world by unimaginable means. He watched videos of the attack happening over and over again. He watched his nation grieve on CNN, ABC, NBC, FOX, and CBS. And while he took no joy in knowing his countrymen had died, he did not feel sorry for the nation itself, for the nation had thrown the world out of equilibrium, and now the world was retaliating. It would all only keep going in a perpetually spinning wheel of violence.

Every American generation before his had some cycle of violence to participate in: the Revolutionary War, the Civil War, World War I, World War II, the Korean War, Vietnam, the Gulf War. When the Towers fell, Jesse saw his generation's opportunity born from the rubble. On September 13, 2001, he enlisted in the United States Army where he would serve as part of the 87th Infantry Regiment, 1st Brigade Combat Team, 10th Mountain Division in Afghanistan.

He learned what everyone learned in basic training: self-discipline, marksmanship, weapons training. But unlike many of his fellow recruits, basic training did not sculpt him. He adhered to its rules; he took from it what he felt it offered him, but he did not fundamentally change. It was what happened in the year after that changed him: he became privileged to esoteric bits of knowledge. For example, he knew exactly what it sounded like when a bullet hit a body. *It's like a fist punching a pillow,* he wrote. *And before that, hummingbird wings.* But it was that punch of the pillow he remembered most.

Jesse was sometimes amazed when he thought about how he had made it back from Afghanistan unscathed. Now, sitting in the living room of his parents' house on Christmas Eve, trying to drink himself blind, he almost wished he hadn't come back at all. It seemed wrong somehow, and he couldn't quite pinpoint why it bothered him. He hadn't wished to die in the highlands of Afghanistan, nor did he wish to die now. But he was apathetic as to the course his life would take. As a cube of ice cracked in his glass of whiskey, it dawned on him: his life meant violence had been cheated out of what belonged to it.

"You might want to slow down on the whiskey, champ," his father said. "There is some beer here, too."

"I don't care much for beer," Jesse said, avoiding his father's eyes as he often avoided others' eyes now.

"Do you want a glass of water at least?"

He shook his head, keeping his eyes on his glass.

"Will you at least look at me?"

Jesse looked up sharply. "There. I'm looking."

Just then Stella walked into the room, holding a tray with three beers. "Aunt Helen's on her way and so is Grandma." She walked over to Jesse and held out a can to him.

Jesse and his father's eyes remained locked as though there were dark matter between them——invisible, dense.

"What's wrong?" Stella put the beer back on the tray.

"Nothing," Gerald said. "There's nothing wrong," and then he walked toward the kitchen brusquely, Stella close behind him.

Jesse thought he could hear his name in whispers from the kitchen, and he was tempted to stand close to the door the way he used to when he was little and his father and mother were engaged in one of their rare but intense arguments. He wondered sometimes if they really loved one another or if they had become so used to each other they didn't know how to live separately anymore. Now that he was older, he decided it didn't really matter anyway, and he didn't worry about his parents much. They were two people he had once known, who had once known him, but he had drifted from them in increasing increments until they barely seemed to occupy the same universe. The space increased more quickly after Jesse's time at war. His father tried to talk to him about it, but he did not want to talk about it with his father who did not know what it sounded like to hear a bullet strike a man and he did not want to talk about it with anyone else either. He wanted to be like the soldiers from World War II had been upon returning. They did not complain, nor did they go around polluting the ears of others with the horror they had witnessed. They had strength, honor, stoicism.

"Gerald, wait," he heard his mother say, but the front door slammed shut and his father's old Toyota started. Then there was silence.

He stood up and walked toward the window, watching his father's car pull out of the driveway. The houses of the neighborhood were all warmly lit, the driveways full. He put his forehead against the cold glass. When he closed his eyes, he saw the houses across the street exploding in slow motion, fire blooming from the windows, shingles and bent pieces of siding flying at high speed toward where he stood. He opened his eyes and then closed them again, watching the show repeat itself.

"Jesse, honey," his mother said. "Are you OK?"

He pulled his head from the glass. "Why do you and Dad keep asking me that?"

"Because you don't seem like yourself."

The neighbor across the street closed his drapes, the living room disappearing until only a small sliver of a Christmas tree was visible, its lights flickering in the gap.

"Maybe this is me. Maybe I wasn't me before."

"I'd like you to see someone. A friend of your father's."

Jesse didn't reply.

"He's a doctor. He's worked with a lot of vets. He's a vet, and he understands what you're going through."

In the silence left behind as his mother's vocal cords stopped vibrating, he heard that familiar sound: hummingbird wings and then the sound of a fist striking a pillow. He snapped around, but behind him was just his mother, her apron smooth and clean.

Silently, he walked toward her and put his arms around her, holding her against his chest firmly, surprised at how small she felt. He kissed the top of her head as she had kissed his when he was a child. Then he went into the dining room and topped off his glass with more ice and whiskey.

His aunt Helen and his grandmother arrived shortly after, and he let them hug him, retaining a cool politeness, and then he excused himself to the garage where he smoked Marlboros in rapid succession, his heart fluttering against the nicotine.

It wasn't part of what was supposed to happen, he had written. *It didn't obey the laws of necessary violence. It wasn't violence. It was cruelty, using the threat of violence to cause fear. Violence is not meant to instill fear. Violence is meant to enforce justice. Men who have nothing gravitate toward misusing violence because they want power. Violence gives them something they don't feel from working or studying or fucking or anything else. They had to dehumanize and humiliate their enemy because they were afraid to be killed and, worse, they were afraid to kill. They should never have been over there in the first place. They weren't made to be, after all.*

"And now it's all ruined," he said aloud to himself. Since he didn't trust anyone with his thoughts, he talked to himself. He held his thoughts much like holding his breath, like the slow darkening around the edges at the top of a suspended inhalation. But he never passed out, and he never exhaled.

"Well, what did you expect?" he said. "Did you expect it all to be wrapped up in a pretty bow?" He laughed aloud, waiting a minute before answering himself. "I expected that we'd be better than that."

The girls there were spent too early. They always had a little dirt on them somewhere. They had eyes like rabbits or squirrels. That's what I remember about the woman: I remember her eyes. I could see them over his shoulder. It was Rogers. I wouldn't have suspected, but I wasn't surprised. He had her up against the outside wall of a house. The scarf covering her head had fallen off. Her fingertips on her right hand were reaching for it. I noticed her hand. Then I noticed that her skirt was pulled up. Her thigh was tan. It almost blended in with the house. It took me a minute to understand. Then her eyes leveled on me, and I saw her terror. Rogers was a fucking terrorist.

When he thought of it now—all of it, the war, the faith he had held in violence—he felt foolish. "So foolish," he said aloud.

The door opened behind him and when he turned around, his father was there. They looked at one another until his father broke the silence.

"Who were you talking to?" he asked.

"I wasn't," Jesse said.

"I heard you say something."

"I just cleared my throat."

"Oh." His father nodded, mouth slightly agape. "Your mother said dinner will be ready in 15 minutes. Do you like the whiskey, by the way?"

"Never met a whiskey I didn't like."

They both laughed a little. It was what his father used to say.

"Listen—about before."

Jesse held up his hand. "It's fine." And for a minute, he did feel fine. The little joke between them made him feel less like someone who didn't belong.

"Did your mother tell you about Scott?"

"Who?"

"My friend that works with vets."

Jesse looked at his drink, the whiskey oily against the side of the glass.

"I think it might be good for you if you talked to him. You need an outlet. It's important. Everyone needs an outlet," his father said.

"I have one." He pulled a Moleskin out of his back pocket. His father stepped forward, and for a second Jesse thought his dad was going to take the notebook from him. He stepped backward, knocking an oil funnel off his dad's workbench.

"Easy, champ," his dad said.

"It's not for anyone's eyes but mine."

"I wasn't trying to take it."

"The hell you weren't."

"Jesus, Jesse. I am not against you. Can't you see I'm not against you?"

Jesse gripped the notebook, said nothing.

"Let's just go eat, OK? Can we have a nice dinner? It's Christmas Eve. Your grandmother and your aunt are here," Gerald said. He walked out as Jesse clenched the Moleskin so tightly his nails made groves in the cover.

Jesse lit a cigarette. He needed to relax before he could go in there with all of them, but it was hard to shut down his thoughts.

I could kill him. I could shoot him in the head, I thought. I could do it without hitting the girl. I lined up my sights on his head. I exhaled. My finger was on the trigger. But she was staring at me. Her eyes were telling me not to. So I couldn't. It would have hurt her more. I didn't give violence what it demanded, and that was my first mistake. I lowered the gun. I walked toward him, and I ripped him off her, his dick waving like a flag. He tripped over his own pants and fell in the dirt. She screamed. And then she kicked him in the stomach and kept kicking him. When she was done, she picked up her scarf and ran away. I watched her calves. They were small and thin. She couldn't have been more than 16.

I leveled the M-4 on him again. I remembered the man in the alley from years ago, the man in the derby cap.

"Pull the trigger, man," Rogers said. "It's the right thing to do."

"There isn't right or wrong," I was thinking. I think I thought it aloud. And then I realized I was not the man in the derby cap or the man in the ski jacket. I was something else.

I was the gun.

After smoking another cigarette, Jesse walked into the dining room where his family was seated, waiting for him so they could eat.

"Saved you a seat, Jesse," his grandmother said, winking.

He smiled at her and sat down, his father watching him carefully. The family passed around plates of ham and dishes of mashed potatoes, cranberries, green beans, and homemade dinner rolls.

"I'm going to put on some Christmas music," his mother said.

Jesse's grandmother rolled her eyes. "That one, always with the Christmas music. Ever since she was a kid. Remember, Helen?"

"She wore out that Bing Crosby Christmas record. I never want to hear that damn thing again."

They laughed while Jesse pushed food around his plate. It was the same story they told every year. It was never very funny; this year he did not find it funny at all.

"I think it's nice," Gerald said. "Your mom is good at being festive."

Helen stuffed a fork full of mashed potatoes in her mouth as "Jingle Bell Rock" rang out from the stereo in the living room. "Real festive," she said.

"Give it a rest, will you?" Stella snapped. But she wasn't looking at Helen. Jesse could feel her eyes on him.

"Girls, do I have to separate you?" his grandmother said.

"Haha, Mom," Helen said. "You're hilarious."

His grandmother set down her silverware, which clanged against her plate. "So, Jesse," she said between chews, "what are you doing now that you're home? Did you find a job yet?"

Jesse shook his head. "Not yet," he said.

"I suppose you need some time to readjust."

He shook his head. "Sure."

"What about college? Are you thinking about taking advantage of the GI Bill?"

Jesse shook his head again. The food was good, and he was concentrating on eating it, on hunkering over his plate. For a second, he floated up over the table and backwards in time so that he was not at the table at all but in Afghanistan, eating an MRE. It was pasta of some kind, and it tasted like the canned pasta his mother had occasionally made for him when she was tired or didn't feel like cooking. He chewed quickly because he wanted to eat it all before he could be interrupted by someone telling him that there had been another explosion, another IED, another near-fatal or fatal injury. Every day it seemed like someone who had once been a human man was transformed into an invalid stump, a hero, whose heroism, in his opinion, would have been better served by death. Heroes died. That was how they became heroes. The rest had to be labeled heroes in order to give them a foothold as they climbed back into a world where they would no longer have a uniform but a disability to set them apart from the rest. Jesse was neither. He had been discharged under Other Than Honorable conditions. There would be no GI Bill or health benefits.

After Rogers had gotten away with what he did to that girl despite Jesse telling superior officers, he lost faith in the military and in its ability to use violence as violence demanded. It all stopped making sense to him. He fought with fellow soldiers. He fought with superior officers. He drank anything he could and took any pills he managed to get his hands on. He did all this until the military no longer wanted him. *There is no shame in freedom. I am a free moral agent,* he wrote.

"I heard on the news that a lot of the colleges are setting up resource centers for vets. You know, to help ease the transition back into college," his mother said. "That might be really helpful for him."

"I heard that, too," his father said. "Definitely could help."

"Can't you give him a job, Gerald? I mean, if he doesn't want to go to school," his grandmother said.

"He can always work for me," his father said.

"I would love it if he worked for you," his mother said.

"Wouldn't that be nice to have both your boys under the same roof?" his grandmother said.

"A dream," his mother said. "It would be a dream come true."

"I bet," his grandmother said.

"I always need help, and I would of course want to pass the business down to him. I've always wanted him to learn it," Gerald said.

"Maybe we should just sit here and plan his life for him," Helen said. "Everyone loves that."

Stella sighed and Gerald set down his silverware and leaned back in his chair. Everyone was quiet for a moment as Jesse ate and ate. "Rocking Around the Christmas Tree" rang out from the stereo.

Finally, his grandmother broke the silence. "Smart guy like you shouldn't have too much trouble anyways, huh honey?"

But Jesse was still far away. He felt the wind come up, and he heard something off in the distance, something loud, and then yelling, but when he looked down, the MRE had been replaced by a dinner plate, filled with portions of all the food he had helped himself to. He looked around at his family who all looked back at him.

"Jesse?" his mother said.

"Jesse, we're all so proud of you," his grandmother said, stabbing a green bean with her fork. "We're all so proud of our hero."

Chapter 15: Las Aves

Months after her mother died unexpectedly of a stroke, Stella felt an uneasiness she could not name. She woke early, tossing and turning in pre-dawn darkness. She thought of all she had not done—the lack of a real career, her unfinished college degree, the fact that she never had a second child. Staring at herself in the mirror, she noticed changes in her skin, new wrinkles, the droop of her jawline. She bought creams and treatments, trying to win back some of what she had lost. At night before bed, she saw her age flashing like a red neon sign, and it sickened her to think of all the years pleated like an accordion behind her.

"I think you should do something," Gerald said, when she finally told him how she felt. "Take a trip. Go somewhere you've never been."

"By myself?"

"I'm sorry—you know I can't leave the business, not now. Take Helen. It would be good for you to be together, especially with all you've been through."

Stella thought about it more and more. She opened the one atlas they owned and looked at maps of the US.

"Not the US," Gerald said, kissing her on the top of her head. "Think bigger. Go to another country." Gerald had traveled to Europe one summer before finishing his undergraduate degree, halcyon days he reminisced about often. "Go see Paris," he said. "Go to Poland where your grandparents came from. Or go to Mexico. You won't even be an ocean away if you go there."

The idea of setting foot on soil so far from home made her nervous, and with Helen, nonetheless. What if they got lost? What if their money was stolen? What if one of them got sick? The scenarios repeated themselves in her mind. Finally, however, she chastised herself. Who had she become? She was far from the woman who left home to be the first person in her family to go to college, far from the woman who drove a drunk stranger home in the hopes of finding love all those years ago. Now she was middle-aged, afraid, and she hated herself for it.

She remembered vaguely her mother around this age. A woman of little means, her mother had begun saving money to have her hair dyed, to take ballroom dance lessons. And it had been a little before this age that her mother left her father. She remembered now the look in her mother's eyes, the woman's eyebrows carefully plucked and drawn in. It was all fire and regret, the light of a storm receding.

"I want to get out of here," she had said. "Out of the Midwest, out of this city. I missed the whole world with an asshole husband and babies on my hips."

Stella hadn't known what to say. She had been one of the babies on her mother's hips. She had weighed her mother down, kept her chained to a place she longed to leave.

That year at Christmas, she and Gerald bought her mother a voucher for travel.

"Go anywhere you want, Mom," Gerald said.

Her mother cringed. "Yeah? With who?" she said.

The room grew quiet. Stella looked at Helen, and Helen looked away.

"Take one of your friends from your dance class," Gerald said.

"Ha," her mother said. "Those old bags? No thank you. I'd rather go alone."

"Then do it!" Gerald said.

"This is what happens when you pick up a husband at a bar," her mother snapped.

She got up and went out on the porch, leaving the door partially open. Cold air and

cigarette smoke flooded the kitchen.

"One of you needs to go out there," Gerald said. "Clearly, I'm not helping."

"Let's go," Stella said to Helen.

Helen threw her napkin down, and they walked out.

Outside, their mother held a cigarette in her right hand, taking long drags from it and staring straight ahead. Her gray roots were beginning to show against the red dye in her hair.

"Mom," Stella started, but Helen put an arm against her.

"What would you like?" Helen said. "If you could have anything?"

"I'd like to go back in time, unmarry your father. Do everything again. You girls don't know." She paused and took another drag. "But you're going to."

One night shortly after Gerald had suggested she take a trip, Stella dreamed she found a small red-winged blackbird lying in the grass. As she held it in her hands, she felt the life go out of it, the bird's body growing cold and then stiff.

"We have to bury it," her mother said.

Helen, looking as she did when she was a teenager, sat in a recliner next to where Stella and her mother stood side by side in their old living room.

"I'll dig a hole," her mother said. She produced a shovel and dug down through the worn carpet in the middle of the room until she hit black earth.

"Here," Helen said, handing Stella a small wooden box.

Carefully, Stella placed the bird in the box and then put the box in the hole. But when they went to cover everything, the carpet didn't fit right over the hole, and parts of the box, of the bird lay exposed. The last thing Stella saw was part of the bird's wing, which shone in the sunlight streaming through the dirty windows, looking as though it could flap at any moment. Then she woke up.

The dream stuck to her all day, her hands remembering life leaving the bird, but she told no one about it and instead let it dissolve like a bitter cube beneath her tongue.

That night, she called Helen.

"I want you to take a trip with me. To Mexico. Will you go?"

For a moment, Helen only breathed.

"You know I don't have——"

"I'll pay for it all."

"I have to think about it. That's so far away. We don't speak Spanish. What if——"

"I'm done with 'what if'," Stella said. "We have to keep living. This is what mom tried to tell us. We can't let anything stop us."

"OK, OK," Helen said.

"So are you in?" Stella asked.

Helen was quiet, and Stella let the silence stand. It was always better to give Helen her time.

"All right," Helen said, and then more quietly, "I'll go."

Stella felt something take flight, and she laughed.

"We're going to do it! We're really going to do it!" she said.

"I suppose we are."

"You'll have fun. I promise. It's going to be good."

"I hope you're right."

They ended the call then, Stella imagining the equatorial sun, clear blue water, and soft white sand.

Two months later, they landed in Isla Mujeres, a small island off the coast of the Yucatan Peninsula. She had chosen the location in part because the flight wasn't long, and the island was small. Stella reasoned that Helen would do better far away from home if she was in a small place. In truth, she thought they both would.

On their first day, they went to the southernmost point of the Island, Punta Sur, where they walked along its rocky coast and watched sea crash into stone as the sun began to set. They stood on Cliff of the Dawn, the place where the first rays of sun hit Mexico every morning, and Stella felt light rise in her. The next couple days of their trip were spent on one of the Island's beaches, known for its calm, sapphiric water. Helen, frightened of the ocean, stayed on shore, busying herself with books and magazines. But Stella swam and swam and swam beneath the blazing sun. Her body was weightless; small fish darted around her as she moved her arms and legs in and out of the salt water. She thought of nothing, not of home, not of her dead mother or troubled son, nor did she think of how age had crept up on her and would only continue to do so. No, she thought only of buoyancy, of air.

At night, she and Helen took dinners in the dining room of their hotel, which was perched on the edge of the ocean. They drank white wine or Aperol spritz, and they stared out at the water, the moon. Tired from their days in the sun, they did not talk much during their dinners, but when they did, it was in the shorthand of sisters.

"Tomorrow?" Stella said.

"I don't care."

"Me either."

"One more drink?"

"Yes."

They slept soundly and late, the way sisters do when they are in the safety of each other.

One day, sunburned and taking a break from the sea, they walked around the little town on the island, which was filled with restaurants and stores. From open doorways, the shops' proprietors called to them, naming what they sold, and Stella and Helen ducked in and out of the buildings at random. They bought souvenirs: t-shirts for Gerald and Jesse, sterling silver jewelry and tequila for themselves. Stella talked with store owners in broken Spanish, while Helen avoided talking to anyone as much as she could.

"You know what I've always wanted?" Stella said as they neared the end of the strip of shops. "I've always wanted a tattoo."

"We're too old for that now," Helen said.

"Says who?"

"Look at your skin."

Stella furrowed her brow. "My skin is fine. So is yours."

They continued walking, now toward the Caribbean Sea, which rushed against rocks and receded, a backdrop of sound to their every step.

"You should get one then."

"How about we get one?"

"Jesus Christ, you really are having a midlife thing, aren't you?"

"We're only going to live once, and we'll probably only ever be here once."

Helen bit her thumbnail a bit, a tell that she was starting to cave.

"Once is enough for me."

"Then let's do something to commemorate it at least."

Helen switched hands and bit her other thumbnail.

"I'll do all the talking. You just have to come with."

"What would we get? I can't think of something I want on my body forever."

"I already have it planned."

"What?"

"Birds."

"Birds?"

"Red-winged black birds."

"Why?"

"Because they remind me of us. They remind me of Mom. And if we get tattoos of them, they'll never die, while we're alive at least."

Helen put her hands down at her sides.

"Don't say I never did anything for you," she said.

Stella threw her head back and laughed. She took Helen by the hand, and they walked until they found a tattoo shop that took walk-in appointments. Later that day, they walked out with their ribcages transformed into aviaries—two perfectly matching birds that could not, would not ever fly away lived in their skin.

"No one is going to believe we actually did this," Stella said.

Rosy-cheeked, they giggled like girls and walked back to their hotel for one of their final dinners on the Island, the birds throbbing like heartbeats against their bones.

When the trip ended and Stella resumed her life at home, she felt different knowing that she had lain on a foreign beach in the sun, that a bird flew silently on her torso. The buoyancy of saltwater lived inside her; all she had to do was think about floating on her back and looking up at the sun.

Chapter 16: British Columbia

On the flight from Chicago to Vancouver, the pilot told the passengers to look out the windows somewhere over Montana. The Rocky Mountains stretched below them, dwarfed by the height at which they were flying. As Gerald stared, his stomach felt what he would call funny, and involuntarily, a lump crept into his throat. Since he was a boy, he had always wanted to see Montana; he associated it with cowboys and horses, with the type of rugged simplicity that he now wished for in life. And here it was, small enough to fit inside a snow globe.

Since being diagnosed with lung cancer a couple days ago, he had been floating. Yes, floating above his own life and peering down at it. Sometimes he wondered if he had already died, if this is what death was, floating and watching, but being unable to do anything about what you saw. He saw his wife but did not feel he could touch her or tell her what had happened. If he told her, he would know he was still alive and that he would have to live through this, submitting to his illness. There would be cards and uncomfortably positive talks with friends, conversations that would only isolate him more. He would wish to hear the mundane details of other people's days, but they would stop talking about that, treading lightly around him. He didn't like change, and with his body changing, the cells multiplying so rapidly, he needed to keep everything outside himself as it was. And so here he sat, flying above Montana under the guise of business travel, looking down at the mountains, on his way to an appointment with a widely-renowned specialist, Dr. Leon, who his regular doctor insisted he see.

"He's a skilled oncologist, and he knows a lot about clinical trials. He always knows the newest drugs and the latest treatments," Dr. Carey, Gerald's internist, had said. "He is the best resource I can recommend for you."

"When should I go? I have to pack, make arrangements."

"I've set this up for you two days from now."

"Two days?"

Dr. Carey nodded. "Two days. I wanted you to get in as soon as possible."

"Two days," Gerald repeated.

Since then, everything had been a blur.

From Montana to Vancouver, Gerald drifted between dreams and when the plane landed, for a few minutes at least, he forgot why he was in Canada and was filled with the type of excitement he got any time he traveled somewhere new. But soon the damp, cool Canadian air jarred him back to reality. He coughed deeply, trying to stifle his hacking as he got into a cab to go to his hotel. He had told Stella he was thinking of expanding his business here before he retired, that he was scouting locations, meeting contacts he had worked with in the past. He was doing it for them; he was protecting their future. While none of it was true, he had constructed the narrative solidly enough that he nearly believed it. Maybe it was true somehow: he was trying to secure a future, or rather ensure that there would be a future.

The first day he went in for blood tests and scans and the day after, he'd see Dr. Leon to review the results. After a pitiful night of sleep in a hard hotel bed, Gerald took a train back to Dr. Leon's office which was in a large futuristic building, the design of which Gerald was sure had meant to signal progress. But inside, the building looked much like any other hospital Gerald had been in: minimalist, sterile, florescent. It carried the same antiseptic stench as all other medical facilities. He checked in with a preternaturally cheerful receptionist and then waited, flipping through some Canadian magazine for the doctor to appear.

Gerald heard Dr. Leon before he saw him. The doctor had a husk to his voice, and his stature matched it. He was tall and broad-shouldered with large hands. Once they began talking, Gerald immediately liked him because like Gerald, the doctor was a man of science, a man who believed fully and whole-heartedly in empiricism, a man who could be neither fully optimistic nor fully pessimistic. Dr. Leon's office was a picturesque physician's study: leather, gold studded chairs sitting at conversational angles; hardcover medical reference books lining the walls behind a large, dark wooden desk; framed diplomas and award certificates hanging on the opposite wall. He poured Gerald a cup of coffee from an expensive-looking machine in the corner.

"I have reviewed all the information from Dr. Carey and looked at all the tests from yesterday. Based on the results of your tests, we know your cancer has metastasized from your lungs to your liver, and it looks like a small tumor has started growing in your brain as well. Treatment must be immediate and aggressive." Dr. Leon put a heavy hand on Gerald's shoulder. "Listen, I'm not going to bullshit you. Even if we start treatment immediately, there is a significant possibility it will prolong your life versus effectively putting the cancer into remission." He took off his glasses and set them down on the desk. "We can also look at clinical trials. I know of at least one you'd qualify for, but it is here in Vancouver, so you'd need to be here regularly for treatment." He paused. "Think carefully about what quality of life you want in the coming months. Talk to your family and decide how to proceed."

"How long do you think?" Gerald clasped his left hand around his right, a hand that had started to go numb off and on over the past few weeks, and squeezed it until his nails dug in.

Dr. Leon looked down at his desk.

"I hate answering this question," he said. "Medicine isn't an exact science. Every body is literally different." He looked back up at Gerald. "But here is what I think based on what I've seen and what I know. Without treatment, you are looking at perhaps six or nine months. With treatment, maybe a year or two. With the clinical trial, we can't say of course, but some of the patients currently enrolled are seeing promising results. Again, you have to think carefully about what quality of life you want. I suggest weighing your options with your family. I'll give you some information to take home."

Gerald released his hand and shook it hard as anger welled in him.

"Can't you tell me what to do? You're the doctor, and I flew all the way up here to see you. So tell me what the hell I am supposed to do." Gerald couldn't see it yet, couldn't see himself as a cancer patient, as a traveler into the kingdom of the unwell——the bald, pale, skinny people he had seen on television and occasionally in the grocery store or on the street. An image of himself hairless with dark circles beneath his eyes flashed in his mind. He shook it off. It didn't make sense; it was not possible.

"All I can do is give you my opinion. It's one that's based on 30 years of experience treating cancer patients. Outcomes largely depend on the person. And what is right for one isn't right for another. Age is a big factor. Older people often decide to refuse treatment and choose palliative care. Younger people, people with kids, usually choose to treat the disease, and of course, they are better candidates. General health, family, all these things play into how people make decisions."

"So what about me? What should I do?"

Dr. Leon smiled cryptically and looked down for a second before meeting Gerald's eyes again. "Look at this like you would any other problem you've faced. Think like a scientist. Imagine the outcomes of each decision and how they will affect you and those around you. Only you can choose what is right for you." He sat back in his chair and stared hard at Gerald. The corner of his mouth twitched for a moment, and then he smiled again. "Listen, my job is to treat cancer. You have cancer. Other than the cancer, at 65, you have high blood pressure and a strong family history of heart disease. I'm concerned about the effects of treatment on your heart. If you want treatment, I'll give you the best treatment I can. We will do radiation and chemotherapy. I can give you drugs to counteract the effects of the cancer drugs. I'll do everything in my power to make you well. What I'm worried about in cases like this is your quality of life. You have to decide if you are willing to be in here or if you want to be out there." He gestured toward the window.

"So that's it? It's that simple? It's just over?"

"Nothing is simple. That's why we create chemicals. That's why man made God. I'm a man of science. A priest would have answered you differently." He paused. "Don't mistake my answer for lack of care or for coldness. I don't believe in instilling false hope in people. I've seen too many broken hearts."

Gerald nodded and looked down at his shoes. Sometimes the worst heartbreaks were the ones where your lover was completely honest, where your lover left you with no hope.

"Think things over, talk to your wife. Come back tomorrow," Dr. Leon said. He cupped one of Gerald's hands in his, the one Gerald had squeezed, and then walked out of the office.

Back at the hotel, Gerald finally looked at his cell phone. Stella had left a message for him. Her voice was smooth and sweet, and he was relieved when he heard her utter his name. For a second, listening to her summarize the simple details of her day, he was able to forget what had just happened, what had been happening over the last couple weeks. He thought only of her, wondering if she was lonely in their house all by herself. He knew he should call her back, but he couldn't, not yet. He needed to be alone. He would make up some excuse later——a late dinner meeting, an invitation to someone's home he couldn't refuse. There was only now, and from here until forever, there would only be now.

Gerald put on a jacket and left the hotel, leaving his phone behind. Once on the street, he took a deep breath and looked around, absorbing everything he could. Standing on the sidewalk in a city he did not know, surrounded by strangers, the world was new and filled with possibility. He turned to his right, and walked downhill, looking toward where he knew land ended and water began.

He walked through the streets slowly, absorbing as much of the city as he could. He took the accents into his own mouth. He added the Steam Clock, the cobbled streets, the Victorian buildings to his geography. He looked at the faces, all the beautiful faces——European, Chinese, Japanese, Indigenous——and imagined all the fucking and fighting and thousands of people it had taken to make just one of those faces. It was amazing, wasn't it? The whole knot of life. The ambivalence and precision of it all. How he was filled with life as he walked! He had not felt this alive in so long, and the altitude of his feeling was directly proportionate to the spread of cancer in his body. He wondered if when the cancer further metastasized, spreading to his bones, he would feel nothing but a prolonged wave of ecstasy. If at the door of death, he would feel life even more acutely.

There was this.

Then there was chemotherapy——hope hung on chemicals.

Then there were the clinical trials——hope hung on experimentation.

There was the inversely proportional relationship between hope and the failure of treatment.

When he reached the waterfront, he stared out over Vancouver Harbor and into the mountains of North Vancouver. Mountains made him feel better. They were wise guardians who cast long shadows. He closed his eyes and breathed out his question so that it caught a wave of air and sailed across the bay into the rocks and trees of the North Shore Mountains.

And he waited for the mountains to answer him.

The next day, he was back in Dr. Leon's office.

"Have you come to decision about how you would like to proceed?" Dr. Leon said, leaning over his desk and pinning his eyes on Gerald's. "Did you talk to your wife?"

"I've made my decision," Gerald said, afraid to say it aloud.

"And? It's OK——take your time. I know it makes more sense in your mind than when you try to say it to someone else."

Gerald nodded. "I don't want to go through the treatment. There's too much to do, and I don't want to spend the last months being in here."

"What did your wife say?"

Gerald looked at his fingernails. They were bitten to the quick, and one had a hangnail.

"Gerald."

He looked up.

"Did you tell your wife?"

He looked out the window.

"Do you love her, Gerald?"

"More than anything."

"Then you need to tell her. She's going to hate you if you don't."

"She's going to hate me for this decision."

"Maybe. But she'll hate you more for leaving her out of it. I find that women are forgiving, except when you lock them out. They don't take kindly to being locked out."

"I won't be able to do a damn thing for her."

"You'll carry her sadness for her."

"What if I can't?"

"You can."

"How do you know?"

"Because everyone I've ever met in your situation is able to." Dr. Leon stood up and walked to the window, his back now facing Gerald. "I'm not religious, and I don't really believe in anything that can't be quantified or measured in some way. But I can't explain the capacity people have to bear the human condition. It's the one thing I can't explain with any sort of measure. You are bearing it right now. And you'll bear her sadness, too. You'll surprise yourself at your own strength."

Tears flowed down Gerald's cheeks, and as they fell, he shed everything, the worry, the fear, and when Dr. Leon turned around, he laughed like a child.

Dr. Leon smiled, and Gerald stood. He embraced Dr. Leon, an embrace that was genuine and strong.

"Into the wild blue yonder," Gerald said.

"Into the wild blue yonder," Dr. Leon said.

"I'll see you again," Gerald said.

"You will. You will."

"Then I suppose I should go."

"One more thing," Dr. Leon said, searching through a drawer in his desk. "This isn't for now. It's for later. And it's just something to consider—something for a man like you."

He put a pamphlet in Gerald's hand. "Put it away for now. Look at it later. Talk it over with Dr. Carey."

"Thanks."

Dr. Leon nodded. Then Gerald was out on the street again. As he waited for the train to take him back to the hotel, he looked at the pamphlet Dr. Leon had given him. *The Final Exit Network,* it read.

Chapter 17: Dreams of Teeth

In a tangle and twirl of cloth, Jesse dreamed of teeth. Cracking teeth. Loosening teeth. Crumbling teeth. In one such dream, when he opened his mouth to the mirror, his teeth were covered in blood. Two of them were loose, and he easily pulled them out. He regarded them, opaque gems, cataloguing their cracks, chips, and discolorations. For a second, he panicked—would he be able to put them back? And if he could, would they stay? Carefully, he slid the first tooth back into place, his gums filled with an angry soreness familiar from the loose teeth of childhood as the root slipped below the gum line. He adjusted the tooth, his hands covered in saliva and blood, until it settled in place. Then he repeated the process with the second tooth. When he looked in the mirror again, the blood was gone, but still, trouble was in his mouth. The dream was so visceral that in his wakened life, he periodically grasped a tooth between his thumb and forefinger at random to make sure it had been just a dream.

Once you lost one of your permanent teeth, it was gone forever. He thought often about that idea—the idea of being permanently lost. As his thoughts drifted before he fell asleep, he conceptualized himself as something that could be permanently lost. Though initially frightening, the idea pleased him the more he considered it. He wanted to wander. Now that the US Army didn't own him, no place should lay claim to him either. *When you wander, you are anything and everything. You are both malleable and rigid. You are both calculable and exempt. You are unclassifiable. You are not a veteran, a hero, a murderer. You are undetected, joining the rest of humanity as you see fit, as it becomes necessary. It is the only way to be free. It is the perfect way of being,* he wrote. *But to be truly free, you need not only to wander but also to be stateless. The state obligates the citizen, not the other way around. Stateless people can't be judged by the merits or misdeeds of a nation over which they have no control. How lucky the stateless, those who live only for themselves and those (if any) that they choose to surround themselves with. That is the way to make the world for yourself instead of succumbing to the will of those who do not care about you.*

Following his discharge, Jesse had grown to hate the United States of America. He hated its hubris, its righteousness. He hated its weapons and the backdoor deals it made to sell them. He hated its politicians with their sideshow rhetoric. He hated all the posturing. But the United States of America was only one nation state in a whole world of corrupt nation states. All of them disgusted Jesse. *If you think people are generally benevolent, put one in charge and others under them. Then watch what happens. Following orders is the most dangerous thing that people do. Trying to belong is the second.*

When Jesse thought about the idea of belonging, he thought of his family, a group to which he had never really belonged. But of all his family members, Helen interested him most. He could not deny that they were both outsiders. When he was a boy, his mother, distraught, had hurried him out of the house to go to Helen's. When they arrived, Helen was sitting at a card table in the front yard of her squat brick apartment building. On brightly colored blankets in front of her were various possessions: books, pots and pans, clothes, furniture. She sipped a bottle of beer as people strolled into the yard, picking up this and that, bartering with Helen over the price of lamps, shoes. Neighbors looked out of their windows disapprovingly. No one had sales on the front lawn.

"What the hell is going on?" his mother said.

"Nice to see you, too," Helen said and then turned away to another customer who wanted a deal. "I can't go lower than $3.00 for that Dutch oven. Sorry."

"We need to talk. Now," his mother said.

"So talk. I'm listening."

"Jesse, go look at Aunt Helen's books," his mother said.

He moved away a little but stayed close enough to listen. "What is this?" his mother said.

"A garage sale. Without the garage, obviously."

"I mean what are you doing? This is most of what you own."

"I'm getting free," Helen said. Her eyes were huge, and she angrily took a pull off her beer. "I'm getting free."

"What is that supposed to mean? Speak normally."

"It means letting go of dead weight."

"This is dead weight?"

"Everything you don't need is dead weight."

"You need help, you know that? You need help. I'm calling Mom. I'm telling her about whatever this is."

Helen laughed, nearly spitting beer out.

"This is funny to you?"

"Yes, it is."

His mother glared at Helen and then "Jesse, let's go," she said. Her face was red, and sweat had gathered beneath the armpits of her cotton shirt.

"Wait." Helen grabbed Jesse's shoulder. "I have something for you. Come here."

"Pawning dead weight off on him?" his mother said. But she waited with her arms crossed as Helen led him away to a box on the other end of the yard.

"I may not see you for a long time, and I want you to have this," she said, putting a black book in his hand.

"What is it?"

"It's a journal. See?" She opened the pages. "The pages are blank. You can do whatever you want in here. It's like a room that you have to yourself. No one can get in. Do you understand? This is a place."

"Thanks," he said. But he hadn't understood yet, hadn't realized the enormity of what she was giving him.

"I may not see you for a while," she said. "I am getting rid of this stuff so I can be free. Things...all these things," she said, gesturing around the yard, "they weigh you down. They hold you back. When you get a little older, you'll know what I mean."

"OK." He nodded at her, not knowing what to say. Then she put her hands on his shoulders and aimed him back at his mother, who still stood with her arms crossed, her mouth in a knot.

They drove home in silence. But later that night, his parents talked about Helen while his mother flew around the kitchen banging pots and pans.

"She's going off by herself."

"Where?"

"She has this idea that she should just go travel around and not own anything. She quit her job. She said she wants to 'get free'."

"What? I don't get it."

"I can't stop her, and this time I don't feel like talking her down. It's her life."

"It is her life," his father said. "And she is going to make of it what she will. But don't you think you should try to talk her down? There has to be something we can say to her."

"I'm tired. I'm just tired. It's been this way our whole life."

His father was quiet then, but Jesse heard something fall to the floor and then his mother crying.

The phrase rang in his head that whole night—*get free.* He opened the journal and wrote it down. It felt good to say it to the paper. So he started saying other things. He wrote about the man with the gun. He wrote his truest feelings, and he continued saying things to paper from then on, and he never forgot the sight of his aunt in her yard with pieces of her life around her. He wished now that he had considered wandering sooner, considered it before going into the military, but there was only now, and he knew what he was going to do.

In the space of a few days, he sold most of his possessions, including all his guns, except for the Smith and Wesson .45, which he would legally carry with him; he sold almost all his books to a used bookstore, some of them collectible editions; and he sold a couch and table, the only furniture that was worth anything, to a neighbor. With each sale, he felt more free, less beholden to a society where he didn't belong. He felt something he had not felt in a long time: possibility.

Altogether, the sales gave him a decent sum—something he could stretch out for a while if he lived cheaply. He still had plenty of savings, which he intended to dip into as infrequently as possible. There was always day labor if his other options failed. He was strong, and he did not mind working with his back, but no one would ever own him again.

The night after the last thing he intended to sell was gone, he decided to drive south to Texas—Galveston, where he could see the ocean. From there, he'd branch out, maybe travel all along the southern border of the US. Going south had always been his plan. He had no use for winter, and if he were somewhere warm, he could camp and wouldn't need to pay for regular accommodations. He imagined campfires and small basic meals. He imagined the jagged peaks of mountains, the rapid rumble of rivers, green rolling hills, and dense forests. He imagined large swaths of unstructured time before him. He imagined his life as a chalkboard newly erased.

In the back of his pickup, he packed his journals, the few books he had chosen to keep, clothes, and other miscellaneous gear. He started the truck and headed toward Interstate 94. As he sped away from all that was familiar, he thought of his parents, who knew nothing of what he was doing. Had he told them, they would have again tried to persuade him to go to college, to take a position at the chemicals factory, to talk to a doctor about the war. The conversation would have been painful for them and frustrating for him, and although he did not feel a close bond with his parents any longer, he did not wish to cause them unnecessary pain. *It's always easier*, he wrote, *to ask for forgiveness rather than permission.*

Chapter 18: The Discoverers

Since returning from Vancouver, Gerald had been insufferable. There had been no lazing about the house, reading the paper, drinking coffee as was their routine on weekends. Instead, Stella had barely been able to keep track of him. He woke before she did and was out of the house just as she was getting out of bed. There was so much to do, he said. But after two weeks of non-stop movement, he finally slowed down. One day before the sun fully rose, she was awake and could sense he was, too. This morning, however, he didn't get up. She reached down and squeezed his hand. He squeezed back.

"Love you," she said.

"You're my favorite girl."

"Better be."

"And you always will be."

"Good."

He turned on his side toward her. "How about I make muffins, the ones with the crumble top?"

"Really?"

"Really. It's been too long."

"I won't say no."

"Then it's settled. You stay in bed and relax awhile. I'll put coffee on."

He slipped out of bed, and Stella turned over and put her arms around his pillow, mapping his path around the house as he moved. First, he would go to the living room and turn on the radio. Then, he would take care of his morning business in the bathroom. Next, he would fill the coffee pot with water and turn it on. Finally, the cupboards and drawers would open and shut as he gathered his tools and then mixed and measured. The only difference this morning was the dry cough that had been plaguing him for weeks.

"I'm sure it's just a dust allergy or maybe the change of seasons, but I'll go in," he had said.

Now she realized she had forgotten to ask him how his doctor's appointment had gone, and he hadn't offered anything up. Had he actually gone or had he rescheduled? She couldn't remember.

When the muffins were ready, they sat at the kitchen table, chewing in silence until Gerald interrupted it. "Let's do something today."

"What do you have in mind?"

"Something different. Something we haven't done in a long time."

"The movies?"

"It's dark in the theater."

"So?"

"So, then I can't see you."

"Oh Jesus," Stella said. "What is with you today? This week. Last week. You're all over the place."

"Let's go into the city today."

"There's nothing else you have to do today—no meetings or anything?"

"No meetings. I'm not going in today. Don't want to. That's the liberty of being the boss." He cleared his throat and swallowed. "Do you remember when we took the boat tour?"

"That was a long time ago now."

"Let's do it again. The city's always changing. There'll be something new to see, I'm sure."

"This early in the year? It's still cold."

"You're a tough bird," he said, winking.

"Seriously, what is with you?" she said.

"I just want to spend time with you."

Anxiety rolled through Stella. For a second, she couldn't swallow the sweet lump in her mouth. "That's all?"

"That's it," he said.

The anxiety rippled away, but she still could not finish eating. "All right. I'll get ready." She put her plate on the counter, concealing the unfinished portion of her muffin in her hand.

A couple hours later, they were walking down Michigan Avenue toward a dock on the Chicago River, the wind whipping around them. Stella told herself that the uneasiness she had been feeling all morning was excitement. It was like they were on a date, and she supposed they were, but they had been on many dates, and their dates had not felt like this for years.

Near the start of the Michigan Avenue Bridge, Gerald stopped abruptly. "I want to take your picture," he said.

"Really? You know I hate that."

"You look beautiful today. I want to remember you right here."

"Jesus."

"Indulge me."

"Fine," she said. "I'll be your model." It had been something else he'd done over the years——taken her picture. He was always taking them when she wasn't paying attention, trying to capture candid images of her, ones in which she didn't have time to freeze in front of the camera. But today was different. Today he wanted to freeze her in front of the camera.

"Stand right there," Gerald said, pointing to a spot in front of one of the bridge's sculptures, *The Discoverers*, which, among others, depicted the famous explorers Louis Jolliet and Jacques Marquette.

Stella forced herself to play along, staring straight into the camera's lens and smiling wide. She put a hand on her hip and threw her head back so the wind pushed her hair out. She laughed and switched poses, blowing kisses as Gerald snapped a few more pictures.

"OK——enough," she said, after she spied people watching them.

Gerald walked to where she stood and put his arms around her. Then he put his hands on her cheeks and kissed her. The kiss ran through her like his kisses had run through her when they were first in love.

"I adore you," he said.

"I love you," she said.

He kissed the top of her head and turned away abruptly. She lagged behind as he walked ahead and then stood silently staring out and across the river as the buildings of Michigan Avenue and Wacker Drive scraped the sky around them. *What is it?* she thought. *What is different?*

"Hey," he said, "do you remember when we tried to take Helen on this cruise?"

Stella started laughing.

"That was the first time a grown woman puked on me," Gerald said, walking back toward Stella.

"Poor Helen," Stella said a little guiltily. "I need to call her. It's been a while since we talked. I worry about her."

"You always do. Just keep at her."

"I will."

"I mean it. You've always taken care of her. You two need to stick together now."

"Why are you telling me that now? We have always stuck together. We're sisters."

"Because you think maybe Helen just needs you, but you need Helen, too. It isn't just one way. And you will need her in the future, too." His voice was urgent; his face darkened.

What is different? she thought. *What has changed?*

"OK, OK, point taken."

"Good," he said, softening. He squeezed her hand but turned his face from hers.

On the boat, Gerald led her to the lower half where they could sit inside and watch Chicago float past them. The tour guide's voice came through speakers, but as the boat began to move, his voice was somewhat muddled, and they easily talked over it. A few other passengers were spread out across the seating area, but there was enough space that Stella felt as though the cruise were just for them. Gerald went to the bar and got them each a glass of champagne.

"Cheers," he said, clinking his glass against hers.

"Cheers," she said, kissing his cheek.

He put his arm around her, holding her body tightly against his. A wave of anxiety welled up inside her again. She pulled away.

"What is it?" she asked. He looked down at his feet and then out the window. Stella followed his eyes, and soon they were both staring at the Wrigley Building. "There's something. I know there's something with you."

"You know that cough I have been having?"

"Yes, did you actually go to the doctor? You didn't say anything, and I forgot to ask."

"I went."

"Well?"

"I went to see Dr. Carey, and you know how I went to Vancouver? Well, I didn't actually go for business."

"What? What were you doing then? I could hardly get you to call me back."

"I've got lung cancer."

"What?"

"Stella, it's lung cancer. I have lung cancer."

Stella's ears rang, and her vision darted every few seconds, like the world had developed a tremor. She took a deep breath and held it, then guided her thoughts into steps.

"What did the doctors say? What do we do next? Did it spread? What are treatment options? There are those special cancer treatment centers . . ."

The tour guide's muffled voice played behind her as she studied Gerald's face. *And*

the . . . Art Deco . . . on the right . . .

"That's what I need to tell you. It's spread. It's in my liver, and it has started to spread to my brain. It's stage 4. I have to tell you, too, that I made a decision about what I'm going to do."

"What decision? You didn't tell me anything." A breeze blew through the boat, and Stella could smell the metallic rot of fish. "You can't make a decision about something like this without me."

"I've decided I'm not going to do anything," Gerald said.

"What? What do you mean not do anything?"

"I'm refusing treatment."

"Like hell you are."

"Treatment isn't going to cure me. So I've made up my mind."

"I can't fucking believe you." She stood up, her champagne glass slipping from her hands and shattering on the damp floor of the boat. She let out a noise, some guttural note of grief, and Gerald pulled her back down and held her tightly. She pushed against him, away from him, but he would not let her go. He released her only when a worker came over to clean up the broken glass.

"We're so sorry about that," she heard Gerald say. But she was worlds away, floating from the boat over the river and toward the sun, which burned her eyes. She thought then of her father, the man who had held her family in torment and disappeared not long after she left college, his evaporation a blessing. When she was still a child, her father had gotten a lucrative construction job, the type of work that had created the boom and bust economy of their family. This job was out of town and would take him away for nearly six months. Though her mother protested, he took the job. During the time he was working in Milwaukee, he had inexplicably been a model provider.

"I don't get it. I just don't get it," Stella's mother repeated while he was gone, running her hands across some new luxury she had been able to furnish the house with. "The man blows his money when he's here and sends it home when he's away. Damn fool. But he's our damn fool, I guess."

Along with money, he'd send letters to Stella, who had just learned how to read. How many times she had read those letters; how many times she had held them to her nose, letting the scent of paper and ink fill her.

Dear Stella,

I hope you are being good for your mom and taking care of Helen. You have always been such a good kid and a good big sister. I've been missing your mom something awful. It's been lonely here without my girls. Kind of miserable. But I'm working hard so I can come home and spoil you girls like you deserve. Going to bring home lots of presents for you. But don't tell Helen. Let her be surprised.

How's school going? What grades are you getting? It looks like your handwriting is getting real good. Bet your mom is helping you. Everyone always said she has such nice writing.

Well, that's about all I can get down here. I'm bone tired and have an early morning tomorrow. Say your prayers and do like your mom asks you.

Love,

Daddy

There were more letters just like that one—nearly a letter for every week he was gone. She had savored the declarations of his affection, for she had rarely heard them before he started sending the letters. No, the father in the letters was a different, milder man, a better man than the flesh and blood father that had left to work out of town months prior. She remembered the time he was gone as happy. It seemed like things were changing, like they were on the cusp of becoming a normal family, and for a while after he was home, maybe they were normal. The father from the letters was the same father there in the house with her and her mother and Helen.

Then, as easily as wind slipping out a window, the father from the letters left. She still remembered when it happened. He had taken to reading her stories before bed after he came home. She would pick a book, scramble up into his lap, and as he read, she followed the words with her index finger, and he'd make up funny voices for the animals in the stories. One night not too long after he was back, she picked out a book and walked over to him as was their custom. When she put her hand on his knee, he pulled his knee from under her hand.

"Can we read?" she said.

He was looking out the window. A car honked its horn. Headlights lit up the driveway at regular intervals.

"Daddy?" She tapped his knee. "Daddy?"

"Can you leave me alone?" he snapped. He stood up, pushing his chair back hard enough that it hit the wall. "I can't fucking breathe in here," he said.

"You're scaring the girls. Please don't be like that," Stella's mom said. "Please."

He was out the door then, the door slamming behind him, and that was that. The father from the letters was gone, and he never returned. She could not reconcile those two men, the father-in-flesh and the father-in-letters. It hurt then and the hurt returned to her now as Gerald revealed his secret, his unilateral decision.

"Stella," Gerald said.

Stella returned to the boat, the sun staining her vision yellow and black.

"Say something to me, please."

It must be like this for Helen, she thinks. Maybe Helen is right: no one ever knows what another person is capable of. No one really knows another person completely. Our hearts are all strangers to one another.

"Every time I think I know you, it turns out I don't," Stella said. "It turns out I don't know you at all." He put his arms around her again, and she stayed stiff, his very musculature foreign to her.

Chapter 19: The Exit Guide

Gerald alternated between perching nervously on the couch and pacing around the living room. Now that the pain was increasing, it was hard for him to be in any one position for a long period of time, unless he was lying down. He checked his watch. Stella wouldn't be home for hours. Still he wished he had arranged the meeting somewhere else, just in case. But the Exit Guide was on her way, and there was no turning back now.

From the sound of her voice on the phone, he guessed she was younger than he was but not that young——maybe in her late fifties. She told him she preferred not to use her real name, that he could call her Sue. Gerald preferred to think of her as The Guide. The title put a halo of light around her, made her otherworldly.

When the doorbell finally rang, Gerald quickly stood up from the couch, throwing himself into a coughing fit. He had to take a detour into the bathroom where he spit out a small amount of blood, something that was happening more often these days. At first, it had been hard to believe cancer was actually inside of him, living and growing, but now he swore he could feel it gaining ground. Every night as he lay in bed, he saw his body as a large map, one that he could manipulate to view from any angle and from any perspective. It was a war map of sorts——a civil war map. Before he drifted off to sleep, he imagined he was on the frontlines, a soldier with a weapon surely too advanced to exist. He used that weapon to bomb and shoot and burn the enemy, to push his foe farther and farther back into the recesses from which it had come. When the battle was over, he slept, but in the morning, the war still raged. The disease regained what he had taken from it the night before.

The doorbell sounded again, and Gerald opened the door. The woman standing on the stairs was thin and blonde and younger than he had imagined. Sunlight played in her hair, and her lips parted to reveal a set of perfect, white teeth. He couldn't help but stare at her a little before he shook himself out of it.

"Sue," she said, putting forth a thin palm with manicured, painted nails.

"Gerald."

"Nice to meet you."

"You, too," he paused, forgetting himself again.

"May I come in?"

"Oh, of course, sorry. Would you like some coffee?"

"Coffee would be great——black."

"OK——make yourself comfortable."

He walked toward the kitchen, turning back once to watch her settle into the couch. He poured her cup of coffee using both hands, as he had grown increasingly unsteady.

Then he headed back to the living room, his steps slow, careful.

"Thanks," The Guide said as Gerald handed her the coffee. "So, I need to see copies of your personal statement and the doctor's statement." She sipped from her cup.

"Sure. I have them right here." Gerald pulled a file off the coffee table. "Dr. Leon, a cancer specialist in Vancouver, is my doctor. He told me about The Final Exit Network and wrote a detailed statement."

"Great. And you've written your wishes as well?"

"Uh, yes," Gerald looked into his cup. The thought of her sitting over coffee and reading what he had written embarrassed him. He had written it late one night over a few pours of whiskey, and the lack of restraint manifested on the page made him nervous. Gerald had always kept his thoughts and ideas close to himself. He wasn't one to philosophize or to proselytize. But on paper his feelings had spilled out easily. *All humans deserve the chance to defeat the illness that feasts on them,* he had written. *All humans should have the right to shield themselves and their loved ones from suffering. I reserve this right for myself: I will leave this life behind on my own terms, at a time of my choosing.*

He stared out the window as she read. He watched the cul-de-sac, the same cul-de-sac he had been watching for years. Mrs. Hudson was pushing her little boy down the sidewalk in a stroller, a black lab by her side. Mr. Frank was working on an old Dodge Charger that he bought for a retirement project. All of it, all of this life, was beautifully indifferent to what was written on the page that The Guide was reading. Gerald took a deep breath, coughed, and leaned back into the couch.

"This is a very eloquently written statement, Gerald. It shows that you have deeply thought through this decision on a number of levels."

"Isn't that what all people do?"

The Guide cocked her head to the side. "Yours is especially eloquent."

"So, what's next?"

"Well, as you know, you have been granted a provisional acceptance. I do have one concern, however, and that concern is your family. We need you to clearly attest that no one will interfere with your wishes. You touch on that in your personal statement, but I think before we talk about anything else, we need to talk about what your family does or doesn't know about your plan. I need you to be honest with me, Gerald. This is undoubtedly the biggest decision you will make. You want to make it without anything to regret in the final moments."

Mr. Frank slammed the hood of his car, and off in the distance, a dog barked.

"Stella——she——Stella doesn't know."

"Is Stella your wife?"

"Yes."

The Guide leaned back and furrowed her brow; the light in her hair made her look like an angry deity.

"And why haven't you told her?"

"Have you ever had a boyfriend that you really cared about but that you knew you were going to have to leave?"

The Guide was silent for a moment. "Yes, right after college. I had to leave for work."

"And you probably kept putting off telling him, right? You just didn't want to tell him?"

"Yes."

"Because you didn't want to sit across from him and watch his heart break, see that look on his face, listen to him cry, right? You almost would have rather just packed up and snuck out."

"Gerald, this is much, much different. You—"

"When I told her that I wasn't going to get treated, I watched her heart break up into tiny pieces right there."

"But it shouldn't be as difficult this time. The shock will have worn off. She may even support your decision."

"No, she won't, and I won't have her know about these plans. I'll write her a letter, and she won't know I've been planning. It's easier that way for both of us."

"So you'll be gone, and she won't have any closure? She's going to feel cheated."

"You don't know Stella."

"Do you?" The Guide asked.

Gerald stood up and looked out the window. No one was out in the cul-de-sac anymore. The houses were still and wide-eyed, the sidewalk empty. He thought of Stella alone in the house, but then he realized he didn't know if she would stay here without him. He simply couldn't imagine her without him or maybe he didn't want to. He felt guilty, but he didn't care because he was dying, and she was living and would continue to live. Having to do all this was torture enough.

"Sometimes I think you get to know someone less the longer you live with them," he said.

"What I'm here to do is educate you about your choices and give advice. I was trained to share all the most up-to-date information on choosing your own exit. But I have to tell you that I have serious qualms about doing that if you haven't been 100% honest with your family. That is not healthy for anyone and could lead to serious hurt. I think we should meet again after you've talked to your wife. After you've talked to her, call me. We'll talk again."

She stood up and moved toward the door. Gerald noticed a tear in the window screen. He made a mental note to fix it before, before—well, before he couldn't anymore. There were so many things left to do around the house. There were still loose ends to tie up with the business, too. The list grew longer as his life grew shorter. The final moments of it? That was a technicality he wanted buttoned up as soon as possible, even if he had to lie in order to get it done.

"Wait," he said. "I'll do it. I'll tell her. Don't go just yet."

"OK," she said. "You're sure?"

"I'm sure."

She sat back down. He continued staring out the window. The flags on his neighbors' houses waved in the breeze.

"What would you do if you were me?"

"What do you mean?"

"I mean, how would you do it?"

"I would move to Oregon, I think. Get a prescription. I'm a nurse, so it's what I'd be most comfortable with."

"I can't move to Oregon." He faced her.

"Most people can't."

"So, what do I do?"

She handed him a pamphlet.

"Read this. It will go over some of your options. One option is bound to seem the most manageable to you."

"I've got options. Well, that's the best thing I've heard in a while."

"That's what being proactive with death is all about."

"Tell me something else, please."

"What's that?"

He paused. He was thinking of his parents, both long dead, who had always seemed like mountains to him. He wished that they were here with him now, wished there was someone before him in line to tell him just to walk forward and everything would be all right.

"Tell me not to be scared."

Her eyes softened. She looked down and then back up at him.

"Don't be scared."

"Thank you for that," he said. "I appreciate it."

"Call me when you've looked over the materials and talked to your wife, OK?"

"Yes, I will."

The Guide let herself out, and Gerald put the information she'd given him in his desk and locked the drawer. He poured more coffee and stared out the window as the sun moved across the neatly edged lawns of his neighbors, whose healthy bodies and beating hearts would continue on long after he was gone.

Chapter 20: The Albatross

As a child, Jesse read a book about a runaway red carpet that was so long it kept unrolling and unrolling from a place called the Hotel Bellevue. He remembered it so vividly, and yet he could not remember the ends of several novels he had read in the last five years. It was funny and sad how that worked. He thought of the book now as he drove south, for he felt as though he were riding that carpet, the fabric unfurling through the flatlands of central Illinois into the Ozarks of southern Missouri. Small worlds were slipping past, galaxies, and he felt like a space tourist. There were so many lives, so many centers, and he was a part of none of them. He was overjoyed; he was elated.

Afghanistan had not been this foreign to him, for he was surrounded by other Americans with whom he was forced to interact with daily. All the soldiers shared something: *We are bound by our lonesomeness and our duty. We are bound by stories of home, and it doesn't matter really how different those homes are. We are all the same here. We are us and not them,* he wrote. It amused him now to think of how quickly that feeling had disappeared once he was back on American soil where he could pull into a McDonald's or Burger King and get something familiar no matter where he ended up.

That first day he kept moving until well after dark and his concentration started wavering. He found a hotel in Broken Arrow, Oklahoma, and checked in for the night, too tired to camp or sleep in his truck. He bought a six pack of beer and drank down two beers before heading to the pool with a third beer in a plastic cup. He stripped down to his boxer briefs and dove into the deep end, swimming underwater until he could hold his breath no longer. Then he back floated, staring at the ceiling, the water covering his ears so all sound was distorted. He closed his eyes and breathed out; he was relieved. Something had ended, though right now he couldn't describe what that thing was. He slept soundly that night, better than he had slept in the past few weeks.

In the morning, he jogged through the streets around the hotel for exercise, stopping at a gas station to get a postcard to mail to his parents. He had cancelled his cell phone service, and he knew his parents would look for him, possibly even try to report him as a missing person if he did not contact them, so he spun the racks of postcards, searching for one that said he was fine, that everything was OK. He selected a two-color card which said, "Everything's Better in Broken Arrow." On the back, he scribbled a short note outlining his plans to travel and then signed it, "Love, Your son, Jesse." He mailed the card and headed back to the hotel. He didn't want to waste anymore daylight in the suburbs of Tulsa with Texas on the horizon.

He had no real logic behind the decision to go to Texas except that it seemed like the fastest way to get to the ocean. He imagined himself landing in Galveston and sleeping on the beach or in his truck facing the ocean so it would be the first thing he saw when he woke up in the morning. From there, he could drive along the coast, maybe even stopping in New Orleans and then heading to Florida, all the way to Key West. When he thought about it, all that air, sun, and water, he was filled with something he vaguely identified as hope, though he didn't know what he was hoping for, except never to feel as he had last Christmas Eve at his parents' house.

As daylight failed, Jesse pulled into Galveston, damp sea air rolling into his lungs. On his way into town, he stopped at a gas station and picked up another postcard. He chose one with cartoonish writing that read "Greetings from Galveston, Texas." On the back he scribbled a few invented details about the sun, the ocean, imbuing each stroke of his pen with an optimism he thought his parents would appreciate. At the end, though it was not necessarily true, he wrote, "I miss you. I'll be home soon." Then he signed it "Love, Your son, Jesse." Satisfied, he dropped the postcard in a mailbox and drove out to the far end of town, where he stumbled upon a small bar, a neighborhood place near the beach called The Albatross. He parked his truck in a lot walked to the bar. Nearing it, he thought of the pistol in his glove compartment but shrugged it off. Why bring it in? Then again, there was no reason not to either. He walked back to the truck and holstered the gun, concealing it under a light jacket. As he walked toward the bar again, he felt better; carrying the gun was right.

The place was nearly empty, black and silver stools abandoned in different directions. A Budweiser sign glowed red on one side of the wooden bar, and a clock hanging over the open bottles of booze was set 15 minutes fast. "$2 Well Drinks, All Day, Every Day!!!" a sign read. On the other side, the Miller High Life maiden hung on a neon moon. The bartender, a young man wearing a backwards baseball cap, approached Jesse.

"What can I get you?"

"A bottle of Bud and a shot of whiskey."

"Rail? Or something else."

"Rail."

The bartender nodded. "Right down to business. I like it."

Jesse gave him a half-smile, hoping he wasn't the kind of bartender who lingered and made small talk about things like sports. When Jesse had his drinks in hand, he turned his attention to the television, signaling he was closed off from conversation. He listened dreamily to the weather forecast: it would be warm and sunny for days. He looked forward to waking in the morning alone with nowhere to be and nothing to do.

After an hour or two, locals trickled in. He felt their eyes on him, but he did his best to ignore it, to ignore the feeling that they somehow knew he was lost. He had gotten further into the whiskey, further than maybe he should have, and as he sank deeper, the nightly news came on, and flashes of troops appeared on the screen. Troops in tan fatigues. Troops smiling. Troops holding guns. Troops being interviewed, their names and ranks spelled out below their faces. Everyone loved the troops. It was taboo not to. *Veteran is a holy word,* he had written. *On the tongue of a nation perpetually at war, it is a holy word.* But Jesse did not believe in holiness, nor did he believe in exaltation. He believed in breath and not breath, in the moment that the heartbeat faded into nothingness. The veteran was merely someone who had the potential to have experienced exactly what it felt like to feel a heartbeat slow and stop by their own hand. A veteran was merely someone who had the potential to bring about equilibrium. That wasn't holy; it was assembly line work in the manufacture of the world. He had grown sick of hearing about veterans, and he had no desire to be identified as one any longer.

"Damn good thing those boys are doing over there," an old man who had just sat down next to him said. The man had white hair, a white beard, and a white baseball cap on. His wiry hair stuck out of the hat at odd angles. "Damn good thing." His speech was slurred and even though they were not facing each other, Jesse could smell his sour, toothless breath. "I served in Vietnam. Two tours."

Jesse stared straight ahead.

"Drafted. Not like it is now. I didn't choose to go. Probably wouldn't have, either. No, sir. Would not have signed up on my own."

Jesse nodded slowly, hoping it would shut the old man up, for he did not want to talk about war—Vietnam, Iraq,

Afghanistan. He didn't want to think about it either. And he hated the fact that after driving for two days, trying to lose himself where the USA met the ocean, he still had to listen to talk of war.

The old man snorted. "Volunteer army," he muttered.

Jesse got up and used the bathroom, intending to find a new place to sit when he returned—a dark corner—somewhere no one would talk to him. But when he finished, there was nowhere to go but back to his seat by the old man, so he sat back down, just as pictures of places both foreign and familiar flashed on the television, places he had been struggling to forget.

"Who gives a shit about this Abu Gharib bullshit? It's war," the old man said, belching under his breath.

Jesse tightened his hand around his beer bottle, as he recalled again the eyes of the woman Rogers had raped.

"Probably got what they deserved." He turned his head toward Jesse. "Right?"

Jesse avoided turning toward him. He shook his head dismissively and kept staring at the television screen.

"Fucking towelheads. I say we blow them all to kingdom come." He nudged Jesse's arm.

Jesse ignored the nudge, closing his eyes and taking a deep breath.

"Make the world a better place, wouldn't it, kid?" The man nudged him again.

Jesse shifted his stool down the bar what little he could. "Will you please shut up?" he asked softly.

"What did you say, kid?"

"I asked," Jesse said, pausing to sip his beer, "if you would please shut the fuck up."

The old man stood. "What in the hell is your problem, kid? You got a problem with me wanting to nuke some terrorists? What the fuck do you care? You one of them?"

The gun was there at Jesse's side, and the muzzle edged against him, prompting him to think about shifting the world closer to balance. That was what moved him—not anger; anger was irrational, sloppy.

"Did I say that?"

"No, but you got some holier-than-thou look on your face."

"Listen," Jesse said, turning toward the man, "I'm sorry. Long day. Let's go have a smoke."

"First you're cursing me and now you want to smoke with me?"

"It's been a long day. I didn't mean anything by it. I'm sorry. I got a fresh pack in my truck. I'll tell you about my time in Afghanistan while we're out there."

"You're a vet?"

Jesse nodded, standing. The man looked him up and down, his expression newly respectful, his lips wet, and his eyes blinking.

"Fine, I'll smoke your smoke, but I don't have time for compassion for terrorists."

The old man turned and walked toward the door. Jesse followed him, his hand on the gun before the door was even shut.

From behind, Jesse pushed the man around to the side of the bar.

"What is this? What the hell?" the man said.

"I asked you to shut the fuck up," Jesse said, bringing the butt of his gun down on the man's nose. Thick blood exploded into the night air and the man stared helplessly at the blood on his hands and clothes. "You were talking about things you don't know about. And you wouldn't stop. I made one simple request." Jesse hit the man again, this time on the side of his head. He fell down onto the shrubby grass and sand and curled his body as though in utero.

"Jesus Christ," the man mumbled. "Please, man. C'mon. I didn't mean anything. I swear."

But Jesse continued to beat him; with each blow, everything came back into balance. What he hadn't done in Afghanistan, he did now.

The man's mumbling stopped, and finally so did Jesse. After, he did not look at the man to see if there was breath left; rather, with righteousness in his steps, he turned and walked toward the meeting of sea and sky. He smelled salt in the air. He tasted salt-tinged iron on his lips. He saw the first stars appear overhead as warmth, waves, and darkness beckoned him.

"Come," they said. "Come home."

Chapter 21: The Wife Hiba

The Mortician learned the rituals of Muslim funerals by accident in Cleveland, Mississippi, a small town that prided itself on staying that way. The town's population included only two Muslims, a husband and wife, the Abdallas. The husband was a professor at Delta State University, a short, neatly dressed man, who excused himself from class when his Middle Eastern studies courses interfered with daily prayers. He did this under the guise of using the bathroom or retrieving a forgotten item from his office, leaving the students to discuss whatever text they had read (or had not read) for that day's lesson. Most often he walked to his office where a royal blue prayer rug with a golden image of Mecca embroidered on it was tucked neatly beneath his desk. But on days when his classes met on the other side of campus, he prayed in a remote, dark corner of the building facing Mecca. This location put him face-to-face with a vending machine as he prostrated himself, knees gracing the tiled floor. It was not ideal, but with little student or faculty traffic, it was the best place to avoid unwanted attention. So, he closed his eyes and imagined himself back in the Baghdad mosque he had prayed in as a boy, a room full of friends and neighbors praying with him, their movements in time.

Of course, the Mortician had known none of that when the man's body appeared at the Cleveland Funeral Home, accompanied by his red-eyed wife.

"He'll be in America forever," she said. "He'll never go home. He always wanted to go home."

The Mortician was quiet for a moment and then "I'm sorry. Just tell me what to do," he said.

"*Ghusl*. I need to give *Ghusl*. To wash him," she said. "And we need white sheets. Can you get them? I need three."

"I'll get you whatever you need," he said, turning to retrieve the sheets.

"There is one more thing."

The Mortician turned back around.

"He can't be embalmed."

"That's OK," the Mortician said, "but he will have to be buried immediately. There might not be time for family to get here."

She nodded, she closed her eyes, and she took a deep breath, squeezing her eyes shut more tightly as she inhaled.

The Mortician stood in front of her until she reopened her eyes and then left to gather the sheets. When he returned, he moved the man's slight body onto the preparation table. The woman began to wash her husband's body, stopping occasionally to wipe her eyes on her sleeve. The Mortician, pretending not to watch, left her to the business of grief, for it was a lonely business, a solitary endeavor.

After washing his body, she shrouded her husband in the sheets, and the Mortician helped her when she asked, quietly following every direction she gave.

"Thank you," she said when it was done. Looking at him, she reached out and squeezed his hand. "*Shukran*. Thank you."

Squeezing her hand back, he felt overwhelmingly that he had done something good, something right.

Now, years later, at Bells & Stone just outside of Chicago, a Muslim woman's body appeared in his preparation room. But this was not any woman. This particular woman had been married to a would-be terrorist, currently serving 30 years in a federal penitentiary for collusion in a plot to blow up the Sears Tower. Those with whom he had colluded had not been fellow jihadists. FBI agents had cajoled him and helped him acquire the very explosives with which he intended to reduce the Sears Tower to rubble. The Mortician could imagine the whole scenario vividly: sweat collecting on the man's brow, his hands wrapped around the detonator, and then the world not vanishing, but only continuing with him in handcuffs. What awful relief!

The Mortician thought it was all dark business: ISIS and Boko Haram and their bends of destruction, their plots, bombs, and guns. But still, he did not approve of young men being pushed, for wouldn't it have been just as easy to push the would-be jihadist in the other direction, to introduce some other way for him to make his mark on the world? Now the man would sit in jail, a consumer of jail food and jail healthcare and jail clothing, until his youth withered. It was a waste of a life——the act of engaging in terror and the act of pushing another to engage in terror.

Though the wife had done nothing but marry this man, others' fear clung to her after her husband's conviction, and its fetid odor trailed behind her. When she died suddenly of an undetected heart defect, the hospital made efforts to contact her family——she had a sister in New York——but no one claimed her. The chaplain at the hospital vowed to keep trying to contact anyone to see to her arrangements, or at the very least, attend her funeral; however, no one came for her, and Bells & Stone agreed to take her body.

Although a Muslim of the same sex was supposed to prepare the body of the deceased unless it was the deceased's spouse, the Mortician took it as his solemn duty to give her the type of burial her faith required; that was, of course, if she had not abandoned it after what had happened to her husband. The Mortician did not understand faith, nor did he understand its child, belief. It seemed so impossible to believe or trust in anything aside from that which could be seen. But this lack of understanding bred in him a respectful curiosity of believers. They all looked so calm. They all looked so happy. At once he envied and pitied them.

Recalling the professor's wife, the Mortician placed the woman's body on the preparation table and said, "In the name of Allah," then began the methodic process of washing her body, avoiding eye contact with its curves and length, even more than he normally did when he prepared women's bodies. When he completed washing her, he shrouded her in white cloth, following as best he could what he had seen the professor's wife do for her husband in Mississippi. Finally, he put a copy of the Qur'an beneath her head so that in death she would rest on her faith.

After it was finished, he walked upstairs, running into the funeral director on the way.

"We have an issue."

"What?"

"The woman down there."

"What about her?"

"It was on the news."

"So?" the Mortician said.

"People found out she's here. They're protesting outside."

"But we don't even know if anyone is coming to the visitation."

"They don't know that."

"Did you call the police?"

"No. The protestors are across the street on the sidewalk, not on our property. I don't think there's anything we can do."

"There's got to be something..." the Mortician started, but the funeral director stopped him, putting a hand on his chest. "You don't need to say it," the Mortician said.

"Are you sure?"

"I'm sure."

The funeral director kept his hand on the Mortician's chest for a moment longer, and the two men locked eyes. Then the Mortician brushed past him and walked upstairs to look out the front windows of the chapel.

Across the street, a handful of people paced with brightly colored signs that read,

Islam Is of the Devil!

Muslims Go Home!

Death to Muslims, Death to Terror!

The protestors chanted; he could see their mouths moving through the leaded glass. While he first would have been inclined to walk outside and try to force them out, today with this woman innocently shrouded in the preparation room, he was more sad than angry, so he pulled the thick blue curtains shut and started walking back down to the preparation room. He passed the funeral director and muttered, "Their God might not judge them, but someone else's will." *That is the convenience of God, isn't it?* the Mortician thought. Human beings were always remaking God in their image so that their actions and intentions became the will of God. For millennia, people had been using God to advance their own righteous agendas. It was brilliant. Blindingly brilliant, really.

Back in the preparation room, the Mortician, not knowing what else to do, sat down next to the shrouded body. The most he could do now was say her name, for although he was sure her name was being said somewhere by someone——perhaps even by her husband himself——saying the name of the dead was a morphemic monument to them, and so as the protesters above uttered their cries of hate, the Mortician said her name in the first degree of audibility above silence: *Hiba.* Gift. And then they waited together for the sun to set, when Hiba's body would be brought to the chapel, where they would continue on together, nothing changed save the venue of their silence.

As darkness tumbled onto suburban Chicago and Hiba's body was transferred to the chapel, the protesters paced outside the doors of Bells & Stone. Inside, the Mortician paced, fearing no one would come to see her. The funeral director, impressed with the restraint the Mortician had for once exercised, had gone home.

At first, the Mortician was able to ignore what was happening across the street, but as time passed and, just like he feared, not a single soul walked through the door to say goodbye, the protesters' voices seemed to permeate the glass and brick of the funeral home. For the sake of Hiba, he tried to keep ignoring them, but they barked and gnashed their teeth, so he walked back and forth with his hands over his ears. Then he switched on the chapel's sound system and tuned the radio to a jazz station, turning it up to an uncomfortable volume, which helped briefly. Minutes later, even though he could no longer hear them above the horns and drums, their presence outside the chapel manifested itself in numbness and twitching in his arms and legs, and an old anger——an anger he had struggled to repress during his time at Bells & Stone, rose in him. Soon he was on his feet and walking toward the door, pausing to pick up a fire stoker from the set of tools in front of the fireplace. Then he was flinging the door open and walking across the street to where the protesters, in their sudden spotlight, stopped yelling and pacing to stare at the man in a suit who marched toward them fearlessly, brandishing a weapon. He stopped just before stepping onto the sidewalk and stared across at their shoreline.

After a requisite moment of silence, he charged them.

"Get out! Get out, you miserable pieces of shit!" he yelled, waving the stoker in front of them. "Miserable bastards! She can't even defend herself! You're as bad as fucking terrorists! Cowards!" The group parted around him so that he stood in the middle of them ranting. A protester charged him, fist raised, but the Mortician swung the iron, striking him hard enough in the arm so that he fell to his knees. A woman came to his aid, glaring at the Mortician.

"Daniel, are you OK?" she asked, as the Mortician spun around, jabbing the poker toward the one or two others who stepped towards him from the safety of the crowd.

"Your God will punish you," he growled. "And if yours doesn't, then hers will. Now go! Get out!" he yelled, letting rage stretch the vowels of his final word.

Slowly, they retreated into the ocean where their particular brand of hatred would blend into the waves from which it had emerged.

Finally, the Mortician was alone, darkness fallen, the iron at his side. "I'm sorry, Hiba. I should have come out here sooner," he whispered into the night. "I'm sorry about it all," he said.

Then he walked back into Bells & Stone where Hiba silently witnessed him packing his personal belongings, preparing to leave the funeral home for the last time. He was sure cops would come; he was sure the funeral director would fire him for what he had done. But that didn't scare him into leaving. Fear had not prompted his packing.

Rather, he realized he had simply spent too much time among the dead.

Chapter 22: Deliver Thyself from Suffering

It wouldn't be long now. But it was hard to pin down the date, the time. It was hard to wake up in the morning and say to yourself, "Yes, this is the day I'm going to die. Yes, this is the very second I have appointed myself to die." Undeniably, however, the beginning of the end had started. The disease had taken control of his body; he was a passenger on an infected vessel. Fluid built up around his lungs and breathing became more difficult. He was often unsteady on his feet, and he was awake and asleep off and on, having lost the thread of circadian rhythm. His body radiated with pain, but he hadn't started taking morphine yet, though he had held the bottle in his hand more than once.

He did his best to feign strength when Stella was around, but she would catch him in low moments, and he could not help but fall onto her breast and take comfort in the familiarity of her body. They said nothing during these times, silencing all the darkness that lay ahead of them. He had not spoken to her of his coming death in any blatant terms. What he had told her as they lay in bed one night was that he had arranged everything. "You'll be taken care of, my lovely," he said. "You won't want for anything. I promise." She nodded silently, and he felt her body grow smaller, but she didn't cry, not audibly at least.

On a Saturday in late September, Stella wanted to go shopping, and though she prodded him gently, Gerald declined the trip. He was too tired, he said, smiling weakly.

"Call Helen. She'll want to go."

"Sure," she said, her back to him.

By the way she said it, he was sure Stella would not call Helen.

She bent down and hugged him, and they lingered over the embrace. He buried his face in her neck, inhaling her so that she was even more a part of him.

"You're my north, my south, my east, my west," she said quietly. It was what she always said to him when either of them left to go on a trip, but now she said it every time they parted.

"I love you," he said. "More than anything."

She stood then and patted him on the head. "Be back soon."

When she was almost to the door, he called her name.

"Yes," she said, turning towards him and looking as he always remembered her: well put together. Her boots, jacket, hat and scarf all matched, and in her winter coat, she still looked something of a girl.

"Did you check the mail?" He was thinking of Jesse again, as he did every day around the time the mail was delivered.

"Yes," she said.

"Anything?" She knew what he was referring to.

"No," she said, and then he heard the door shut quickly.

He felt the letdown he had felt nearly every day since they received Jesse's last postcard a few months earlier. They had no way to contact him, and therefore, the fact that Gerald might never see his son again became more real every day.

While Stella was gone, Gerald went into their bedroom and then into the recesses of their walk-in closet. It was here that he had been stowing the tools of self-deliverance: the "Exit Bag," a special plastic bag with a Velcro collar, plastic tubing, and a nitrogen tank. The tubing on the Exit Bag hooked up to the nitrogen tank, and when he released the valve, nitrogen would fill the bag, depriving his body of oxygen, and rendering him unconscious. He would die within minutes.

He laid the equipment out on the floor and carefully ran his fingers over the Exit Bag, the tubing. He regarded it the same way he did a loaded gun: with reverence, with fear. He picked up the bag, and with a horrible tear, pulled the Velcro collar apart. Slowly, he put the bag over his face, and then secured the Velcro strap shut. When it was in place, he turned one step at a time until he was facing himself in the mirror. The bag expanded and contracted as he breathed. The air inside of it grew warm and moist; his heart raced.

Consumed by wild anger, he tore at the bag until finally he was free, coughing, gasping for air, and silently cursing all that cancer was going to make him do.

The day would be soon, he knew, but it would not be today—not when he still occasionally had good days. As carefully as he had unpacked everything, he packed it again, and hid it in the darkest part of the closet, the part where once a dead mouse lay undetected for so long that the smell of its decomposition came and went before they found it.

On days when he felt more well than others, his mind lured him into a velvet untruth, and he imagined perhaps he was just getting better—like the day on which a stomach virus broke and his mother made him scrambled eggs, tea, and toast for his first meal. These days he spent with Stella, and on these days, he baked. Whereas he used to bake by himself often while Stella was sleeping or out, these days he baked with his wife. She let him lead her around the kitchen, assign her various tasks, and stand behind her, guiding her hands as she kneaded the dough.

"Sourdough," Stella said. It was 6:00 a.m., and they had both woken in the early dark.

"Is there still starter?"

She leaned into the refrigerator, removing containers until she discovered it in the back. "Found it!" she said, her face alight and almost giddy.

He laughed; finds so small always caused her joy.

"We need one cup."

She carefully measured out a cup and put it into a bowl.

"Tell me again about the starter."

"I will if you measure out two cups of bread flour and put them in this bowl."

"Does this mean I don't have to knead?"

"If you're good," he winked at her.

"Now tell me how to do the starter."

"Every time you use a cup, you replace it with a cup of flour and a cup of water. And if you don't use it but you want to keep it going, you just throw out a cup and replace it. You can freeze it to, but I always just keep it going."

"So it just keeps going and going and going."

"It just keeps going and going. I originally made this batch a month or more ago. You will just want to keep adding to it."

Stella looked at him, her mouth open as though she were going to say something but then decided not to. Sensing what had stunted her speech, he turned his eyes from her to the dough, kneading it until all the flour was mixed in and none of the dough stuck to the sides or bottom of the bowl. Then he put his dough-covered fingers behind his back and kissed her on the neck, the cheek, the forehead until she smiled.

Silently, they settled in at the kitchen table with cups of coffee as the loaf of bread rose and the starter fed on the new flour and water, a living, breathing thing.

Over the next couple weeks, as his pain and difficulty breathing increased, Gerald woke routinely in the middle of the night, sweating, his heart pounding, signaling he was on the edge of something, as though he just made the decision, as though his sweat and racing heart were signs letting him know he had done something irreversible. When he tried to fall back asleep, he saw only his face behind the plastic bag. Worse, he imagined Stella walking in and seeing him like that, ashen and suffocated, already far away.

On a Wednesday a few weeks later, rain fell steadily all morning. Stella and Gerald lay in bed and listened to it until well past the time they usually got up. Finally, Stella broke the spell and said she would make coffee. She stood and pulled on her robe, and Gerald intended to follow her, but as he tried to send his legs over the edge of the bed, every inch of his body responded unanimously with the same droning note of pain.

When she returned with two cups of coffee, he did not intend for his face to show what he felt, but it was impossible to hide it. She stopped short. "Should I call Dr. Carey?" she asked.

"Come here," Gerald said, and while he had never intended to tell her, he knew he would tell her now, and he knew with certain clarity that she would understand.

"Today's the day," he said.

"The day?" Her face transformed into that of a child's whose half-knowing never stopped her from asking questions.

"Today."

She sat down on her side of the bed and did not face him; instead she gazed out their bedroom window, which looked out onto a row of backyards, all of them the same shape and size, all of them unpopulated save the few puddles that had accumulated from the persistent autumn rain.

"But the yard, the gutters, the basement——Gerald, I'm not ready."

"You know then."

"I know you."

"How do you know?"

"I found the kit. You always leave the closet door open after you do something in there, and I guess——I guess I just had a feeling something was back there or there was something you hadn't told me."

"Lay with me."

"I don't want to."

"Lay with me."

"I don't want to, Gerald. It's the first part, isn't it? The laying with you."

"Do you want to be here, Stella?"

"Do I have a choice?"

"Of course."

"Do you need me?"

"Stella, we've never needed each other."

She turned her head, and he could see the steep slope of her Polish nose.

"It was always want with us, wasn't it?"

"Yes. That's why we have what we have."

"Do you want me, Gerald?"

"Yes. Always."

"Good."

"Then lay with me."

Stella said nothing, but simply turned toward Gerald and put her head on his chest and her arm around his waist as had been their custom all these years.

"Helen can live here with you," he said. "You need to keep taking care of her. You've always been the strong one. It'll be good for you both to be together."

"It isn't right, Gerald."

"What isn't right?"

"All of it. None of it's right. This wasn't the way things were supposed to happen. And Jesse now—what about him? What will I do?"

"You'll do what you've always done."

"Which is what?"

"You'll get through. Jesse'll get through. He'll have to come out the other side eventually. He'll come back to you."

"Who's going to take care of me?"

"You are."

"But you've always taken care of me."

"And I still will be taking care of you. Even when I'm not here. I've made sure of it."

"It just seems wrong. It seems like you're giving up. Why are you giving up? Why did you give up?" she said flatly, running her hand over his chest.

"I'm not giving up. I'm beating it, Stella." He coughed deeply.

"Does it hurt?" she asked.

"Yes. It hurts. But I'm beating it."

"I don't understand."

"As long as I stick around here in pain, that cancer is just going to keep growing. It's a parasite."

"I don't understand."

"Yes, you do."

"I don't want to."

"Help me beat it."

She said nothing but squeezed him more tightly. It hurt, but he let her hold on. They lay like that until Gerald broke the silence.

"You aren't asleep, are you?"

"No." She shifted her body. "Is it still today?"

"Yes."

"Why? Why today?"

"Because today is different. Today is the start of worse days. Today is the day that the good days stop."

"You are my north, my south, my east, my west," she said.

He kissed her forehead. The rain had stopped; stray drops fell from the trees. An occasional bird called from the feeder at the back of the yard.

"Are you sure you'll stay?" he asked.

"I'll stay if I'm wanted," she said.

"You are." He squeezed her hand, and she smiled, her eyes watery and opaque. "It's going to go quick—just a few minutes once we start. If you need to, just look out the window."

"I won't," she said.

"When it's done, call the ambulance. Tell them you found me like this. Take the car out first. Drive around the block so the engine's warm and don't put it in the garage, then call."

"OK."

"Kiss me."

They kissed, and when their lips parted, Gerald nodded at her.

"I'm going to get a drink of water," she said, but she sat there for a second before she got up and walked out.

"OK," he replied, and thinking of what lay in the corner of the closet, he tried to stand, but again, he was unable.

Stella came back in the room with her water. "I was just thinking about that ice tray we had when we were first married."

"The one we couldn't get any ice out of?"

Gerald laughed and Stella put her head against his for a moment and they laughed together the nervous way they always did when they were about to do something they had never done before.

They stared at each other for a minute, and Gerald put his hand over Stella's. "Stella——I can't," and then he nodded toward the closet.

"Oh," she said. "What if I don't?"

"But you will."

"Will I?"

"I know you love me, and so you will."

Stella turned toward the window again. "Mr. Frank put a for sale sign on that car."

Gerald said nothing.

"I suppose now he'll just buy another one."

"I suppose."

Gerald realized that after today, there would be no one for her to have such a conversation with. For a second he thought about changing his mind, but then imagined another day of not being able to get out of bed and another and another. He imagined soiling himself. He imagined lying in bed half-conscious, Stella rubbing ice over his lips. He imagined his body holding on, his mind completely taken by tumor and morphine. He imagined, as he had read about, scratching himself in pain though, unable to tell anyone he hurt.

"Stella," he said.

She got up and walked to the closet and a moment later returned with the kit. She put the Exit Bag on Gerald's chest and then pulled the tank close to the bed. Gerald held her arm and pulled her down to him. "I love you," he said. "Now just forgive me for anything I've ever done to hurt you, and I'll forgive you, too. No loose ends."

"I forgive you," she said. "I love you. No loose ends."

Gerald turned on the small CD player on his nightstand. The song "Blue Velvet" wrapped itself around them as Stella turned away from him and he dressed himself in the Exit Bag. When she turned toward her, he nodded at her, and she lay next to him holding his hand, her head on his chest.

He reached his hand to the tank and opened the valve. He breathed deeply, he closed his eyes, and he concentrated on the melody of their song and on the terrain of Stella's hand, mapping valleys and peaks he had not yet catalogued. Soon, instead of mapping them, he was traversing them, ambling through terrain at once both foreign and familiar. It was all plush, it was all lovely, and the last thing he thought was that he was so happy.

Chapter 23: As Dense as a Void

In her small life, Helen had taken to going for long walks alone, often seeking water, as water calmed her. Since she had spent so much of her life ill at ease, now that she was growing old, she wanted only to feel easy. There was a pond in a park that she frequented. It wasn't much to look at it—some ducks trudging among random pockets of litter—but still, when she closed her eyes, she could feel the wind blow off water. Small fish swam in the shallows. Frogs congregated in the long, wet grass on the shore. Red-winged blackbirds darted in and out of the cattails. She liked thinking of all the life surrounding the water, life indifferent to the human condition, and most days, that was enough to settle her mind.

It was when she returned from one of these walks that she got a message from her sister. In the message, nothing but the urgency in her sister's heart came through the machine. Helen immediately dialed Stella's number.

"Gerald's dead," was all Stella said when she picked up. Helen knew it was going to happen—they all knew. Still, she hadn't thought it would be this soon. The last time she saw Gerald, he looked fine, but then she remembered the way he paused before standing up from his recliner, his mouth pinched, his brow furrowed as he struggled to lift himself. When she left, sooner than she had planned, he hugged her more tightly than normal, squeezing her hand before she pulled away. She could still see them, Stella and Gerald, in the picture window of their living room, standing together, watching her back out of the driveway. She remembered thinking something about them at that moment, something that may have been cruel. What was it? *Such a perfect pair. If I was your kid, I'd have been out of here, too,* she had thought. It was mean; she shouldn't have thought it, and she wasn't sure why she did. They were the type of parents she wished she and Stella had. Cheerleaders, mentors. Plus, they had money. They provided everything for Jesse that she and Stella never had access to. So why did she think that? She had been jealous because she lost her sister to an interloper, but after reluctantly accepting Gerald, she was no longer jealous of her sister's attention to Gerald but jealous of them, of the looks they exchanged, the way they seemed to have had made love stay, even after all the years of marriage.

Now she was ashamed of her jealousy, her pettiness. Stella had lost her one true love, and Jesse was nowhere to be found. What had she done? Was all this suffering her fault? Had she made this happen by thinking such horrible things?

"Helen?" Stella said, interrupting Helen's thoughts.

"I'm sorry," she said, "I'm so, so sorry. I'll be right over."

"Can you bring me some cigarettes?"

"Of course."

"Will you stay?"

"Yes, I was already planning to."

"Good."

Helen hung up the phone, grabbed an overnight bag, and thinking better of it, pulled out a small roller bag. She threw in enough clothes for a few days and then her toiletries. She grabbed her favorite blanket, a pillow, and sleeping pills and put them in her overnight bag. And then, for good measure, she put the couple bottles of wine she had in as well.

She turned off all the lights, locked the door, and packed up her car. Inside her car, she looked at her building before starting the engine.

Nothing will be the same now, she thought. Then she turned the key and drove away, faster than she should have.

At the house, Stella was sitting on the sofa drinking chamomile tea and smoking a long cigarette. All the windows were open, and a cold wind ruffled a copy of *National Geographic* sitting on the coffee table. The cover featured a picture of some tropical locale, and Stella's eyes were fixated on it.

"What happened?" Helen said, dropping a fresh pack of cigarettes on the table.

"He did it," she said, closing her eyes and blowing smoke out the window. "Had it all planned out. I didn't even know he was planning it. He didn't tell me. Nearly 40 years. Nearly 40 years of marriage, and he didn't tell me anything about his plan. It was just like him, I suppose. I shouldn't have expected anything less."

"What exactly did he do?"

Stella turned to her sharply. "You come over to get the dirty details?"

"No—I'm just..."

"Curious? You always were the macabre one in the family, weren't you? Always wanting to know all the dirty details of everything. Always the one holding up traffic to stare at a crash, trying to see if there's blood on the concrete. Who wants to see Mom's body put into the crematorium? Helen does. Of course. Anything morbid. Ask Helen."

"Jesus, if you don't want to tell me, that's fine." She reached out a hand to her sister's shoulder, but Stella shrugged it off.

"I watched," she said. "I held his hand until he wasn't holding mine back." She stood up and started shutting the windows. "He'd be mad if he knew I was smoking again after all this time. Smoking in the house, at that." She slammed each shut harder than the last, and when she returned to the living room, tears were running down her face.

"You know he got someone else pregnant before Jesse was born? A woman named Sarah. The baby died. She used to write him letters, and he never told me. He never told me any of it. Fucking asshole."

"Come here," Helen said. "He didn't mean it. Come here." She recognized what was happening in her sister, and she knew though Gerald may have kept secrets, though

Gerald wasn't perfect, he was good. It was easier to be angry than to be sad, and her sister was just so sad. Anger would never take that away.

Without saying anything else, Stella lay down on the couch, putting her head in Helen's lap. Helen rested her palm gently on her sister's head. When Stella didn't protest, Helen rubbed her hair the way their mother had when one of them needed soothing.

"There, there," she said. "There, there. It's OK. It will all be OK."

Stella gripped Helen's knee, and her body shook as hot tears streamed from her eyes. Tears welled up in Helen's eyes, but she held them back, knowing she needed to be strong for her sister.

"He loved you so much," Helen said. "He just loved you so much. Everyone knew. It was so obvious." She kept rubbing her sister's hair, the hem of her dress soaked with Stella's tears. "He may not have always done what you wanted him to, but he was always thinking about you. He wanted you to be happy. That's all he wanted."

Stella nodded her head slightly and squeezed Helen's knee twice.

In that moment, the absence of those they loved filled the room, and though the sun shone brightly, the room was as dense as a void.

Chapter 24: Still Life

When it was all over, the funeral, the cremation, Stella kept waiting for the back door to open. Like one of Pavlov's dogs, she expected it at dinner, as she had always been home cooking before Gerald walked in. Sauté and boil and fry as she might, she could never conjure Gerald from the fog of culinary heat. Nor could she fathom how the life they had lived would fossilize and become part of photo albums and recollections.

Do you remember when Gerald was convinced he could bake that wheat bread over the campfire? Do you remember when Gerald made those amazing cinnamon rolls? Do you remember? Do you remember?

That was all there was: things Gerald had *done*. He would not do any more things, which was the hardest for her to accept because she still imagined him wrapping an arm around her waist and asking her what he could do to help prepare their evening meal. She could still smell him in the lingering musk of Barbasol that somehow arose in the steam from the shower. When the bright red cardinal shone against the bare branches of the tree in their front yard, she could only imagine it was him, peering in the front window, watching over her, their house.

But those were the only ways he was there. In several other ways, of course, he was painfully absent. His bulk was not curled in their flannel sheets at night. He did not eat the leftovers, which, without his hunger, simply rotted. He did not yawn or fart or belch or shit. All the things that bound him to human life had vanished.

A couple months after Gerald's death, Stella realized that Helen hadn't been to her own apartment in a week. The number of possessions she kept at Stella's had grown until it seemed everything she owned, which wasn't much, was there. Stella suggested that she just move in since the house was big enough for them both. Without Stella asking twice, Helen broke her lease, packed up her apartment, and settled herself in Stella's house.

Over the next year, their lives assumed an easy routine of Rummy 500, light dinners, and the occasional visit from family or friends. They took walks in the mornings and evenings and visited rivers, lakes, parks. They watched birds. They grew chard, tomatoes, squash, rosemary and tried new recipes. They made pasta and sauce from scratch. They bought kits and made their own Pinot Noir. They traveled to California, Arizona, Florida, fleeing the frigidity of the Midwest.

But there was one person who was painfully absent: Jesse. The only proof Stella had of his continued existence were the two postcards he had sent—one from Oklahoma and another from Texas. It had been well over a year since any word had come from him. Having no other way to contact him, she sent a copy of the program for Gerald's funeral and one of the last pictures he and Gerald had taken together general delivery to Galveston, Texas. In the photo, Gerald's arm is around Jesse, and they are both smiling. Jesse leans on a shovel, and they stand in front of the garden they had just dug out for Stella. Like most pictures, this picture lied, too. It was one peaceful moment frozen in a tumultuous sea. But perhaps that was why people loved pictures so much: pictures allowed them to remember things in pleasant little stills instead of candid motion. Stella hoped sending it to Jesse might motivate him to make good on his word that he would come back soon, that it might grab him by the heart and say,

There were good times, yes, there were good times here. But instead, the package arrived back in her mailbox a few weeks later.

When the package came back, she stared at it, turning it over and over in her hands. All she had wanted was to see her son, the most important link she had to Gerald, but now she did not know if she had a son anymore. He hadn't been well before he left; they all knew it, but there was no stopping Jesse when he was set on a thing, and really, he hadn't given them much of an opportunity to stop him anyhow. Now, nights when she couldn't sleep, she stood by the window the way she used to when Gerald worked late and watched the road for headlights to illuminate the pavement, signaling someone was coming home. Each time the pavement lit up, she felt nauseous, and her heart quickened, just in time to see the car rumble into someone else's driveway. Sometimes she'd turn around, and as if Helen's own body felt what hers did, Helen would be standing behind her, holding a cup of tea out to her and saying something that had nothing to do with why they both knew Stella was standing at the window. For this, Stella was grateful. Hers was a ritual meant to be private.

The day after one of these nights, the sisters had dinner guests—some friends of Stella and Gerald's—and after dinner, one of the guests asked to take a picture of the sisters. In the picture, they were standing in front of Stella's old China cabinet, which was full of their mother's wedding dishes, figurines, collectible spoons, things they had both lived around so long that the items had lost their individuality. Stella and Helen's arms were around one another and Helen, as it had been her habit since she was a child, leaned into Stella, who had always been taller and sturdier than she. They both smiled, and the camera's flash bounced off the glass behind them, which created a single point of light between them in the photo. They hung the picture on the refrigerator, and there it stayed while they cooked their light dinners, played their games of Rummy 500, and entertained their guests.

Looking at that picture, one would see two women who shared a resemblance, two women who had carried the flickering light of their forebearers, two women who had wanted as all do before simply accepting what they have, two women who had led somewhat unremarkable Midwestern lives.

But, then again, it was only a picture, a happy little still.

Chapter 25: Portraiture

After fleeing Bells & Stone, the Mortician's life transformed from the vivid color of silence to the black and white of sound. The living talked too much. They went on and on. They protested until you paid attention to them. They asked things of you.

"Excuse me," they said. "Can you tell me what time it is?"

"Would you like another drink?" they asked.

"Can you fill this application out and return it by tomorrow?" they said.

"Have you dedicated your life to the Lord Jesus Christ?" they queried.

Even when he wore his headphones, the Mortician seemed to hear the living more acutely than he had before—or perhaps without the silence of the dead, the living seemed so much louder. He had not expected losing the dead would have this effect on him, but still he found himself irritable and depressed. This was compounded by the fact that he had moved from Illinois to Minnesota, the farthest north he had ever been. The night he prepared Hiba, after leaving Bells & Stone, he started driving northwest, through Wisconsin, until the twin cities of St. Paul and Minneapolis unfolded before him in the light of early dawn. He thought moving north would make him feel freer, but it did not. He was trapped by his past, by the uncertainty of his future, even though he was far away from one and the other was his to shape. With only a modest amount of savings, no job, no marketable skills other than mortuary science, and no idea how to remedy any of those ills, he was overwhelmed. Encircled by choice, he stood in the center and looked around and around until he was too dizzy to pick a direction to follow.

Having secured a cheap studio apartment in Stevens Square, a small neighborhood in Minneapolis full of apartment buildings and old houses in various states of disrepair, he took comfort in visiting the Minneapolis Institute of Arts, a large, admission-free museum. Walking through the galleries of paintings, photographs, and sculptures was much like being around the dead. Rembrandt, Van Gogh, and Matisse all contributed to the architecture of silence. The art asked nothing of him. It was a relief, a reprieve from the noise of the living. Most importantly, the museum had given him a direction to follow in the form of a girl, *Portrait of a Woman* by Jean-Baptiste-Camille Corot.

On one of his early trips to the museum, he first saw her. *Portrait of a Woman* was an oil painting no bigger than the size of the front page of a newspaper. In it, a woman sits outdoors in the countryside, perhaps at dusk. Only her profile is visible, her dark hair pulled back tightly. Her lips are taut, her eyes downcast, her clothing simple and brownish gray. A dark scarf is tied around her neck. She is a plain woman, an ordinary looking woman, but he had seen many plain and ordinary women and learned they were not what they seemed. They had secrets: stories, tattoos, lines of joy and sorrow. The woman in this painting, too, was anything but ordinary.

When he stared at her, as he had taken to doing, he felt as though he were sitting just slightly behind her and to her right. Even as he stared and imagined being in the painting next to her, he never felt she would turn toward him or speak to him. They were merely alone together. For the Mortician, who was used to being alone while with the shells of others, the portrait of this woman was enough company for him. Many mornings, he drank a cup of coffee in the museum's café and then walked into the small gallery where she hung in the center of a white wall, a dim light shining on her. He sat on a bench across from her, closed his eyes, and imagined he was in the world of the painting with a breeze blowing, the scent of grass and wood in the air. He imagined how a piece of the woman's brown hair might suddenly spring loose from its knot and blow behind her ear. He would lean closer and closer to her until that same piece of hair brushed against his cheek, his nose, filling him momentarily with her scent.

The longer he stayed with her, the harder it became to leave. It seemed unfair, really, that she should have to remain in this museum, guarded by young, pot-addled, tattooed men who, having become so used to her presence, simply passed her by without even stopping to acknowledge her. Their lack of attention frustrated him, and he tried to suppress his frustration by telling himself that these young men had many pieces of art to watch over, that they couldn't commit to spending time with her. But had he been a guard, he would have spent time with her; he would have found some way, some system to spend time with each of them, all the mute and beautiful frozen faces.

One night after having spent his morning with the portrait, he imagined where he would hang her in his apartment if she were his. He imagined her in the living room over the brick fireplace, which no longer worked. He imagined her in the small dining room, hanging opposite the window where the morning sun would warm her face. Then he imagined her hanging on the wall across from his bed so that her face was always the first and last thing he saw. As his thoughts drifted and floated toward sleep, he saw himself walking into the museum, taking her off the wall, and walking out with her. He saw himself bringing her home for the first time, and then, just as his body jerked back from the beginning of a dream, he opened his eyes and thought he could see her on the wall in front of him. He sat up straight, then realized what he saw was not her at all, but just the alternating light and shadow of a car driving by.

He pulled himself out of bed and poured a glass of whiskey to calm his nerves. At the bottom of his second glass, he knew what he wanted, what he was missing, and what he had been searching for. He would find a way to make it happen; he would do it no matter what trouble it brought him. He would bring *Portrait of a Woman* by Jean-Baptiste-Camille Corot home with him.

It won't be that hard, he told himself. *Confidence. It's all about confidence.* He had confidence. It had kept him employed. Conversely, it had also gotten him fired. He didn't allow himself to think of that now as he packed a navy blazer and red, navy, and white striped tie into a messenger bag. He wore a white shirt and gray pants with plain black tennis shoes, which, having spent enough time at the museum, he knew would successfully disguise him as a museum guard—at first glance, anyway.

Having arrived at the museum rather shortly before close, he was able to find a parking spot on the street on the side of the building. It wasn't ideal, but it was as close as he could get without parking in the ramp. He took a deep breath and looked to his right at the white face of the museum. Its columns stood strong and impenetrable, and the front was lit with an array of colored lights. His stomach turned at the thought of what he was about to do, but then he saw her face in his mind and imagined the sheer relief he would feel when she was in his arms. The end of loneliness was in reach.

He put on a baseball cap, pulled it low over his face, and walked into the museum where he nodded quickly at the man working the desk at the entrance. Then, to pass the 30 minutes before the museum closed, he browsed through the collections he already knew well: the Impressionists' paintings, the period rooms with their carefully preserved luxuries, and an exhibit of photographs centered on immigrants. He kept a close eye on the guards, who quickly appeared and disappeared. A few times it seemed a guard was following him——a large man with unkempt black hair——but he dismissed the suspicion as nerves and kept a controlled pace. He was tempted, of course, to go to her, but he did not let himself. Like a nervous lover waiting for his beloved, he checked his watch too often as he paced around the museum. During that time, he was never tempted to turn back, not once.

Soon it was time for him to retreat to the bathroom where he would hide as the museum closed. On his way to the bathroom, in one of the Modernism galleries, a guard smiled at him and said, "The museum will be closing in 10 minutes, sir." The Mortician kept his head down, avoiding the guard's eyes as he turned the corner that would lead him to the men's room. At the bathroom door, he looked to his right and to his left, but he saw no one, so he opened the door and slipped inside. Thankfully, it was empty. He removed his baseball cap and splashed water on his face, slicking his hair back. He looked himself in the eyes, finding he had no problem doing so, which only affirmed he would have no regrets after whatever happened when he walked back into the museum. He went into the stall at the end opposite the entrance and pushed the door nearly closed behind him. He climbed up so that he was sitting on the toilet tank with his feet on the seat and waited for a sign that the museum was officially closed.

When a guard finally came in about 20 minutes later, the Mortician held his breath as the man surveyed the bathroom, peering beneath the stalls.

"Anybody in here?" he said. "Hello? Anybody?"

A muscle in the Mortician's calf cramped suddenly, and he shifted involuntarily, causing a subtle squeak in the toilet seat.

The guard stopped. "Hello?" he said again. "Is someone in here?"

The Mortician watched the man's feet move toward him, waiting for the door to his stall to spring open. But then the guard paused in front of the mirror. Through the tiny sliver of open stall door, the Mortician watched him lean forward, inspecting something in his reflection. Finally, he looked around once more and then walked out. The Mortician exhaled when the door closed and then put on his tie and blazer to match the guards. It was time to go where she silently hung, waiting. He walked back through two of the Modernism galleries, past a full-size replica of a glowing silver car and then into Gallery 355. His heart pounded; his tie felt like a foreign hand squeezing his neck as he neared her. Every inch of his skin was alive, alert.

Once in front of her, his pulse slowed. He felt as though he had just walked up from the coffee shop, bits of breakfast pastry still in his teeth. *At last,* he thought, *we'll be together. You and me.* Tears gathered in his eyes; he stared for a moment before shaking himself into action. With delicacy, he pulled her off the wall, expecting an alarm to sound.

But to his surprise, no alarm sounded.

She was much lighter than he had expected. For a second, he was so entranced with her that he forgot what he was doing until a noise in another gallery jarred him to action.

He wrapped her in his raincoat, holding her next to his chest, and walked quickly but quietly, stiff-legged and determined, back through the Impressionist galleries, past the photography exhibit where hundreds of eyes silently witnessed his crime. As he grew closer to the exits on the main floor, he saw a guard. The guard's back was turned towards him, and he was talking on a cell phone.

"Yeah, sure, I'll pick up cat litter on my way home," the man said, turning in time to see the Mortician walking through. He stared at him for a second, but then nodded and put two fingers up in a wave.

"I know, I know. I'll see you soon," he said into the phone.

An emergency exit was nearest to the Mortician. He knew an alarm would sound when he opened the door, but this was the closest way out to his car, so he prepared himself to run. *Ready?* he asked the woman in the painting.

Ready, she replied.

Let's go, he said, bracing her more tightly.

He shoved the metal door open, and an alarm rang out. He sprinted as fast as he could across the museum's lawn to his car. He jumped in, carefully putting her in the front seat next to him. He closed his door just as two men ran toward him, their mouths and arms moving frantically. But he and his license plate were cloaked in darkness, and he squealed away, leaving the men breathless in his wake. He laughed and laughed until his stomach hurt, and the woman in the painting laughed, too. *We made it!* he said. *We really made it.*

It was a stroke of luck that the museum was near the entrance to two freeways. He had a choice of which to take, I-35W or I-94E. As he flipped on the headlights of his car, he asked the woman in the painting *Which way should I go?*

You choose, she said. *I want you to pick.*

He nodded, but he wasn't sure what was right, and so the Man Who Was No Longer a Mortician looked at the point of her chin—a compass which he imagined would point him in the truest direction—and bade his car to follow.

Acknowledgements

For feedback, support, and patience as I shaped this book, I'd like to thank Emma Alice Johnson, one of my early readers. I'd also like to thank my husband, Tanner Servoss, for reading a draft of this novel well before he became my husband and lending his keen editorial eye to it. Many thanks also go to the incomparable writers Linda LeGarde Grover and Raki Kopernik for their willingness to read the book. Rain Newcomb and Anna Fellegy, two great friends, helped me make this book shine. I've been blessed with wonderful teachers in my life, namely Karen Loeb and the late Charles Russell, who never stopped believing in me. Their support and guidance have been invaluable. I am also so grateful to Unsolicited Press for believing in this book and in my first book. Finally, I'd like to thank my family: my late father, from whom I inherited a love of reading; my sisters Amirah, Lisa, Yvonne, and Linnea; my brothers Mike and Craig; and my dear aunt Janice. I was born lucky.

About the Author

Darci Schummer is the author of Six Months in the Midwest (Unsolicited Press) and co-author of the poetry/prose collaboration *HINGE* (broadcraft press). Her work has appeared in *Ninth Letter, Folio, Jet Fuel Review, Sundog Lit, Pithead Chapel,* and *Necessary Fiction,* among several other journals and anthologies. A Pushcart Prize and Best of the Net nominee, she teaches writing at Fond du Lac Tribal and Community College where she also serves as faculty editor for *The Thunderbird Review.* Connect with her at darcischummer.com.

About the Press

Unsolicited Press is based out of Portland, Oregon and focuses on the works of the unsung and underrepresented. As a womxn-owned, all-volunteer small publisher that doesn't worry about profits as much as championing exceptional literature, we have the privilege of partnering with authors skirting the fringes of the lit world. We've worked with emerging and award-winning authors such as Dan Gutstein, Shann Ray, Amy Shimshon-Santo, Brook Bhagat, Kris Amos, and John W. Bateman.

Learn more at unsolicitedpress.com. Find us on twitter and instagram.

9 781956 692969